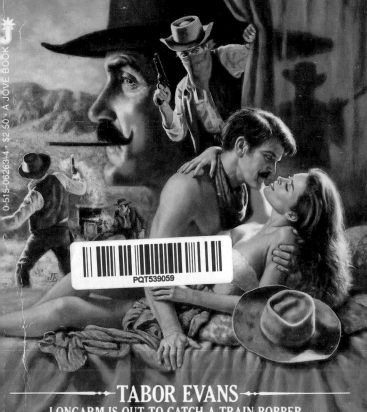

PQT539059

◆ TABOR EVANS ◆

LONGARM IS OUT TO CATCH A TRAIN ROBBER—
AND A FIERY LADY JOURNALIST
IS OUT TO CATCH HIM!

62

LONGARM

IN VIRGINIA CITY

0-515-06263-4 • $2.50 • A JOVE BOOK

Millicent laughed and let out a short yip of happiness.

"What was that about?"

"What was it *about?* Silly man. Why, you have just guaranteed, I mean positively *guaranteed,* that I will be able to sell a story, finally. And, I might add, in the meantime I get to make passionate," she fondled him, "and frequent love to a *real* U.S. marshal."

"Just a deputy," he corrected.

"Don't quibble, dear." She bent over him, her falling hair tickling the insides of his thighs. "Not at a time like this."

What the hell, Longarm thought. It was tough duty, but someone had to do it.

Also in the **LONGARM** series
from Jove

--◆-→◆ **TABOR EVANS** ◆←◆--

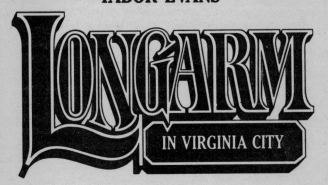

IN VIRGINIA CITY

A JOVE BOOK

LONGARM IN VIRGINIA CITY

A Jove Book / published by arrangement with
the author

PRINTING HISTORY
Jove edition / January 1984

ISBN: 0-515-06263-4

Jove books are published by The Berkley Publishing Group,
200 Madison Avenue, New York, N.Y. 10016. The words
"A JOVE BOOK" and the "J" with sunburst are trademarks
belonging to Jove Publications, Inc.

Chapter 1

Longarm walked jauntily down the sidewalk whistling a very well remembered light melody. It was only nine o'clock, but already he had been to a barbershop for a shave, a trim, and a generous application of bay rum toilet water. His stovepipe boots gleamed with a fresh coating of hard wax, and his tweed coat and trousers had been brushed to perfection. The day was bright and glorious, the air so clear it seemed to magnify the range of mountains lying to the west of Denver and make them look like they were near enough to reach afoot in the forenoon.

The night promised to be even better.

He was smiling and still whistling as he passed the gray stone exterior of the Denver Mint and turned up the steps of the federal building. It was almost a shame he did not encounter anyone on the sidewalk. He felt so very good that he wanted to share the high humor with someone. Anyone. *Everyone*.

The tune he was whistling was the one Brenda Savoit had been singing the night before. That had been the first time he had heard the song. He did not think it likely that he would forget it.

He smiled again, and his eyes softened with memory and anticipation.

Brenda Savoit. Lovely as the songs she sang. Golden hair in a mass of ringlets. Face of a cherub, round and sweet. Figure like . . . well, Longarm was still guessing about the figure, although the theatrical tights she had been wearing gave him a mighty good indication of what he could expect in the very near future.

He sighed.

Last night had been only a prelude.

He had been seated front row center thanks to dumb luck and a favor owed, and he had been sure that the lovely girl's eyes had singled him out during her appearances on stage.

It was most unlike him. He was no dang Stagedoor Johnny to fall all over himself for the suspect charms of an actress. But this girl had seemed different. Different enough so that he abandoned his own habits and stopped backstage afterward to pay his compliments.

The gesture had been welcomed and the invitation plain. He had gone with Brenda and the others in her touring company for a late supper after the show.

It had all been quite proper. Miss Savoit had not offered to so much as hold his hand under the table. But there had been much more than hand-holding promised in the looks she gave him. And there had been an invitation to another, private supper late tonight after their evening's performances.

Damned if Longarm was not really looking forward to his second delightful meeting with the beauteous Brenda.

He was grinning when he swept into U. S. Marshal Billy Vail's outer office. He hung his Stetson on the rack, gave the clerk on duty there a hello, and went on back into the marshal's private office without waiting to be announced. He was still whistling Miss Savoit's melody.

"*Good* morning, William." He grinned at his boss and helped himself to a seat, turning the straight-backed chair

2

that had been placed in front of Marshal Vail's desk and straddling it.

"You're feeling chipper this morning, I see. You are also late." Vail pulled an American Horologe from his vest pocket and consulted it to confirm that his deputy was indeed checking in past the usual time for the start of working hours.

Longarm's grin did not falter. He knew as well as anyone that Billy Vail was not the kind of incompetent political appointee who went by the manual and nothing else. Vail was a former field man who had achieved his position the hard way, and he was more interested in results than in punctuality. Yesterday Deputy U. S. Marshal Long had returned from Durango with three prisoners after a week-long chase. If he was a touch late reporting in now, it was no major problem.

"Don't tell me. Let me guess," Vail said. "A woman, right?"

Longarm's grin got wider.

The marshal leaned forward. His nostrils twitched. The movement also caused the sunlight coming in through the window behind Vail to reflect off the man's balding scalp. Longarm did the prudent thing and refrained from mentioning that fact.

"Must be quite a woman, too, since you were willing to pay extra for all that stinkum," Vail said.

"Quite," Longarm agreed.

Vail leaned back in his chair, removing the halo of sunlight from his dome, and steepled his fingers under his chin. "I hope you didn't have plans for tonight."

"But I do."

"No, you did," the marshal corrected.

"What?"

"No free meals at the public trough, Custis. You have to earn your keep, you know. Duty calls."

Longarm groaned. Then be brightened and he sat up straight again as a thought came to him. "You got a telegram yesterday afternoon, right?"

"Indeed I did."

Longarm's grin returned to his tanned face. He had been in the office the previous afternoon when the message arrived. Senator Titus Hardee's brother, sister-in-law, and niece were arriving today, and the senator had asked the Justice Department to provide them with a courtesy escort for their "personal safety" in this uncivilized wilderness of Denver. It was the sort of perk a good many swelled-headed politicians demanded for themselves and was, Longarm privately thought, entirely too normal.

Still, he could show them whatever they wanted to see—probably the wilder the better if past experience gave him anything to judge by—and with any luck at all he could have them tuckered out and tucked soundly into their accommodations before Brenda's last show ended. So all need not necessarily be lost.

This was not exactly the kind of duty a man signed on for when he took up a deputy marshal's badge, but it was something they all had to put up with from time to time.

"No problem, Billy," he said. "I'll make sure the senator's family sees us as they imagine us to be out here in the Wild West."

"Senator's family? Who said anything about that?"

"But..."

"I've assigned Randall Edwards to that one," Vail said.

Longarm's face fell.

"Don't be so disappointed," Vail said. "The sister-in-law is obviously married, and the niece is only eleven. You aren't missing out on anything. Besides, Edwards has a daughter about that same age. The choice seemed appropriate."

"But..."

"Your assignment?" Billy said. "Don't tell me we actually got a message into this office without you seeing it before I did. Surely not."

The marshal paused as if waiting for another protest from his best deputy, but by now Longarm had gotten the idea

4

that he might as well wait and listen instead of jumping to yet another erroneous conclusion.

Vail smiled. He looked, Longarm thought, remarkably like a bald, pink-faced tabby with a ring of small feathers caught in its whiskers.

"This *other* telegram," Vail said, stressing the word 'other,' "was from Kyle Lewis in Cheyenne." Vail's expression changed. He looked serious now, and Longarm got the distinct impression that playtime was over. "I've been at the Western Union office half the night, actually.

"It seems an informant popped in out of the clear blue in Cheyenne yesterday and told Lewis about a planned robbery—a very large robbery—in or near Virginia City. Since the plan calls for it to be a train robbery, Lewis thought it should come under our jurisdiction. Mail coaches and so on."

Longarm nodded. Jurisdiction was always a consideration, and Kyle Lewis as town marshal of Cheyenne would have scant excuse to get into anything under federal control despite his reputation as an honest lawman. Longarm knew the man and liked him. He respected him too, which was not something he could always, or even often, say about local lawmen.

"It seems this informant spun his tale and then hurried away. Lewis might not have attached much credence to his story, but the man turned up again at the Union Pacific depot a few minutes later as the object of a homicide report. He was standing in a crowd on the platform, presumably waiting for a train either arriving or departing, when someone slipped a knife into his back. Lewis's impression—and I agree with it—is that the murder tends to strengthen the man's believability. Of course, we have no idea whether the robbery gang knows he had already tipped the law or if they think they got to him in time. If he was seen at Kyle's office, they will naturally go underground with their plan and be harder to locate."

"Virginia City, though, Billy. Hell, there's a U. S. Marshal right there at Carson City, isn't there?"

"There is," Vail agreed, "but I believe I mentioned that I've been sending and receiving wires all night long."

The deputy noted that the amount of time involved had doubled since it was first mentioned, but he knew better than to say anything about that at the moment.

"Two things," Vail said. "One is that the District Marshal there . . . and, frankly, Longarm, I don't know the man; he could be very good, or he might just as easily be some knothead sucking the taxpayers' tit . . . says he is too short-handed over there to handle this himself. Apparently one of his men resigned recently and another one is sick and everybody else is just plain busy, or some such balderdash. For all I know, he might not want to be bothered with a crime that hasn't been committed yet."

Longarm grunted. That was a piss-poor attitude, but one that was not entirely uncommon. It was, he supposed, one of the primary differences between an officer who wanted to think of himself as a law enforcement man and one who would rather be thought of as a peace officer. Given a choice, Longarm would much rather be a peace officer than a lawman. Keeping the peace whenever possible seemed a much better idea to him than catching someone between the hammer of a badge and the anvil of the courts.

"There was a second thing?" he asked.

"You are paying attention. Good."

Longarm let that one slide.

"The second thing," Billy Vail said, "is that you already know our alleged would-be train robber. If we are going to assist with this—and it looks like we will have to, if anyone is going to get around to doing the job—you are the logical choice, Custis."

Longarm sighed. He couldn't help thinking, briefly, about Miss Brenda Savoit and her still-hidden charms. "Who?" he asked wearily. Funny, he didn't feel like whistling any more.

"Professor T. Anthony Scott," Billy said.

6

"The Professor? Forget it, Billy. The informant was full of it. I brought the Professor in myself not—oh, four years back. Something like that, anyway. Mail robbery that time too, but he was sent to Leavenworth for twenty years. You can't rob a train from a cell in the federal pen, Billy. The tracks just don't route through there."

Vail shook his head. "That's the second time today I've caught you not knowing as much as you thought you did, Longarm. While you were down south last week we got a flyer in on the good Professor. It seems he managed to get away from Leavenworth about three weeks back. He killed a guard in the escape, so this time he hangs when he's caught."

Longarm made a face. "The son of a bitch is smart, Billy. He wouldn't be easy at the best of times, and with a hanging to face he's going to be even harder to take."

"I know, but that too seems to make this robbery information make sense. It's reasonable to think the Professor would want to make one big haul at what he does best, which is robbing trains, and then get the hell out of the country."

"Why Virginia City, though? That's not near any border."

"That's where the bullion is. The Comstock is the biggest strike this country has ever seen. And from there he could take a train across to California and then head south to Mexico easily enough."

Longarm shook his head. "That doesn't sound right to me. Not for the Professor. Some grubby little Mexican village wouldn't be his style."

"South America, then."

"Not for him. The man likes to put on airs, you know. Europe would be more like it, I think."

Vail smiled. "See? I told you you were the man for this. That's exactly the sort of thing we need to know if we hope to catch him before he can make his score and skip."

Longarm sighed. He might as well put Miss Savoit com-

7

pletely out of mind now. Unless he could make a quick arrest of the son of a bitch and get back here to Denver in one large hurry. The troupe had a two-week engagement at the Hanson House, and they had only been playing there for three days. With any luck . . . but there was time to think about that later.

"Is there anything else I need to know, Billy? The Professor was always one for disguising himself, so I won't necessarily recognize him even if I bump into him."

Vail smiled again, but there was no humor in the expression this time. "It gets worse, actually. I asked the warden at Leavenworth for particulars on the Professor while he was a guest there. According to the rather brief telegram I got back this morning the Professor acted as a model prisoner while he was there and participated in several dramatic productions staged by the inmates."

"Jesus, if the son of a bitch has learned about makeup too I really might be able to have a drink with him and never recognize him."

"You're the best chance we have, Longarm. I already told Kyle Lewis that you'll stop by his office on your way to Virginia City. You have to go through Cheyenne to get there anyway, so you can stop and get filled in on what the informant told Lewis, then be on your way west on the next train out."

"I'll have to stop by the rooming house to get my gear," Longarm said. "It's packed and ready to go, of course."

"Take a hack and charge it to your expenses," Vail offered. "I want you on this right away, Custis."

He nodded and wondered if that offer would extend to having the hack driver take a message to Miss Savoit as well. No, he decided; better to pay that out of pocket. Damnit.

"I better be off then." He unwound himself from the chair he was draped over and stood.

"Custis."

"Yes?"

8

"Keep in touch, would you, this time?"

Longarm grinned at him. It was one of Billy's pet peeves. No matter how often one of Vail's deputies telegraphed progress reports, the man was never satisfied. Longarm often had the sneaking suspicion that Billy still thought of himself as a field man and was probably convinced that he could have done a better job if he'd been out there himself.

"I always do," Longarm said happily, and escaped through the office door before Billy Vail could offer a retort to that perfectly obvious untruth. There were times, in fact, when Deputy Marshal Custis Long took a positive delight in twitting his boss by remaining silent during the course of an investigation. Not that he would withhold information. He would not think of doing something that might jeopardize the job he was assigned to do, and a man never knew when unexpected circumstances—like knives, clubs, or bullets—might make it necessary for another deputy to step into the middle of a job only partially done. But damned if Longarm was going to go out of his way just to say howdy three times a day, the way Billy would have liked them all to do.

Longarm paused at the top of the federal building steps to light a cheroot, then hurried down into Colfax Avenue in search of a hack.

Chapter 2

There were four occupants of the Cheyenne town marshal's office and city jail when Longarm arrived. Three of them were behind bars. The fourth was a youngster barely old enough to require twice-weekly shaves who was sitting behind the marshal's cluttered desk with his boots propped up where they would leave bits of dried mud on the wooden surface. He was wearing a badge, so Longarm assumed he must belong there.

"Afternoon," Longarm said politely.

The kid's eyes widened, and his boots left the top of Kyle Lewis's desk to thump down onto the floor. He looked nervous when he sat upright in the swivel chair, and he seemed to be paying a good deal of attention to the Winchester that rode in a boot tied to the McClellan saddle that Longarm was carrying in addition to his travel valise.

Longarm ignored the young deputy and dumped his gear into a corner of the office. He could have left it at the depot and hired a boy to look after it or simply trusted the station man, but lately it seemed more and more difficult to know who a body could trust. These days he preferred to keep himself responsible for his belongings when at all possible.

"Who are you?" the deputy asked.

Longarm reached into his coat pocket for his badge, and the youngster visibly started. He looked relieved when Longarm pulled out a wallet instead of a gun.

"Deputy United States Marshal Custis Long. I believe I'm expected."

The youngster slumped back into the chair with a sigh.

"If you've got something to be that jumpy about, son, you shouldn't wait to see what a man pulls," Longarm advised. "I could've shot you if I'd wanted."

"Yes, sir." The boy licked his lips.

"On second thought," Longarm said, "you look nervous enough that you'd best stay away from your gun unless you got a real good reason. You don't want to go around shooting innocent citizens. What's up?"

The deputy motioned behind him toward the cells. "Them back there, sir."

Longarm raised an eyebrow.

"They're part of the Calder gang, sir. Them and the Calder brothers killed an old couple stayin' in the hotel a couple days ago an' robbed them. Marshal Lewis, he caught these ones here, but everyone's saying they're gonna be busted loose by the Calders before they can hang. When you come in, well, I thought maybe . . ."

"Where is Kyle, boy?"

"Out after the Calders, sir. He got a tip they'd been spotted up around Torrington and he tooken off after them with a warrant."

"Damn," Longarm muttered. "I need to see Kyle before I head west."

"You're outta the Denver district, sir?"

"Yes."

"He told me he was expectin' a depitty from down that way an' said I was to fill you in when you got here if he wasn't back his own self."

That was something, anyway.

11

Longarm took a closer look at the boy. He did not seem like the kind of good officer like Kyle Lewis would choose to employ. Surely Cheyenne couldn't be that hard up for good men. "Who's your daddy, son?"

The deputy smiled shyly. "Mayor Alfred Perkins, sir."

Longarm grunted. That explained that, then. "What do they call you, Deputy Perkins?"

"Perk, sir. My real name's Alfred Ray Perkins the Third, but everybody calls me Perk."

"All right, Perk, you can call me Longarm."

"Yes, sir." Perk smiled again.

"Mind if I sit down?"

"Oh. No, sir. I'm sorry."

Longarm sighed and took a seat next to the desk. He pulled out a cheroot, took his time about trimming the end, and lighted it. "Now, what is it you were supposed to tell me, Perk?"

The boy thought hard for a few moments before he answered. When he spoke he gave the impression he was repeating something he had learned pretty much by rote.

"The informant's name was Mel or Mal, no last name given. He said he used to run wild an' knew some of the Perfessor's men but he'd gone straight. They tried to recruit him to join them for a job. A real big job. There's s'posed to be a gold shipment the end of the month. A real big one. The Perfessor figures to take it. Him and a pegleg man called Duck an' Al Higgins and Leroy Tyler an' maybe some others. The informant didn't know how many there was supposed to be, but he was sure about them. They figger to take the gold as it goes out o' Virginia City an' make a really big haul. Marshal Lewis, he said to give you the flyers we have on Sidney Bragg, known as Duck or Sidney Duck, an' on Al Higgins. He said to tell you this Mal, or Mel, was positive that the robbery's to be the end of this month when the moon'll be right an' that they're all set on it except for maybe a little more muscle."

Deputy Perkins thought a moment more, then sat back

12

with a nod. The message had been delivered in full.

"What about the murder of this informant?" Longarm asked. "Do you know anything about that?"

"Yes, sir, I was there for that one, though I hadn't seen him when he talked with Marshal Lewis before. I went down to the depot with Marshal Lewis an' I seen the corpse myself."

From the sound of his voice Longarm guessed that young Perk was not entirely used to the sight of corpses.

"He was knifed in the back," Perk went on. "Slick as greased ice, it was. There wasn't no fuss and nobody heard him squawk. Somebody seen him slumped over on the bench and figgered at first he was just drunk, but then they seen the blood on the bench and sent for us. He was dead when Marshal Lewis and me got there."

A cold, silent killing like that, Longarm thought, was damn sure no mere flareup over a drink or a woman, the kind of thing men usually died from when they were not sick in bed. It pretty much had to be a planned murder of the sort that would certainly, as Kyle Lewis already believed, lend weight to this Mel's, or Mal's, story about the Professor and his gang.

Longarm accepted the Wanted posters Perk handed him. They took only a moment to read. Sidney "Sidney Duck" Bragg was a one-legged man of approximately forty, heavyset, with scars and burn tissue on both hands and forearms. He was wanted for bank robbery in Oregon and was known to be expert with explosives.

Just how expert Bragg was Longarm was skeptical about, since the flyer also mentioned that the loss of his leg and the burns were caused by an accidental discharge of blasting powder some years earlier. Maybe, Longarm thought charitably, that was before he became such an expert.

The poster on Al Higgins was even less detailed. Higgins was wanted for second-degree murder in Deadwood, Dakota Territory, where he had killed a man with his bare hands.

Bounties were set at $150 for Bragg, fifty dollars for

Higgins. Longarm had never heard of either of them before, nor did the name Leroy Tyler stir his memory. Apparently there was no paper out on him, at least not under that name.

Longarm tossed the posters back onto Kyle Lewis's desk and stood. "Thanks for your help, Perk."

"You aren't leaving, are you?" the boy asked.

"Sure. It's hard to say when Kyle might get back, and there's a westbound scheduled in forty-five minutes. I intend to be on it." He hesitated. "Is there any reason I should wait?"

Perk shook his head nervously. "I expect not, sir. I was just hopin' you'd stay till Marshal Lewis was back." He looked over his shoulder toward the jailed members of the Calder gang. "You know."

Longarm smiled. "No point in worrying until you have cause, son. There's a whole lot more talk about jailbreaks than there are jailbreaks." He tugged his Stetson lower on his forehead and crossed the room to reclaim his gear. "Remember, Perk, it takes a pretty cowardly bastard to rob an elderly couple. The kind of man who'd do that isn't likely to take on a gun-carrying deputy in broad daylight. So don't you worry about it, hear?"

Perkins smiled uncertainly. "Yes, sir, I'll try an' do that."

"Okay, boy. Good luck to you."

Longarm hoisted his saddle over his left shoulder and walked out carrying his valise in his right hand. He had given the young deputy what he thought was perfectly good and valid advice, but long habits of caution kept him from burdening his gun hand at any time. If he should happen to need to reach the double-action Colt .44-40 that rode high and forward over his left hip, it would be no trick at all to drop the bag and get the weapon into action.

That, though, was an ingrained caution. He had no reason to think he would need the Colt until or unless he caught up with Professor T. Anthony Scott in Virginia City. And then, with any luck at all, he would be able to have things under such complete control that firearms would not be necessary.

Longarm sighed. He always *wanted* things to work out that way. It was a shame that they so rarely did.

He stepped into the slanting light of the late afternoon sunshine and nodded politely to a well dressed man who was mounting the board sidewalk from the street.

"Howdy." The man disappeared into the marshal's office, and Longarm smiled slightly. Deputy Perkins would feel better with someone there for company, he was sure. The kid sure was a worrier. Longarm turned toward the depot and lengthened his stride. He wanted to make sure he had plenty of time to get a bite to eat before he boarded the westbound coach for Ogden and the change of trains on toward Virginia City. Meals aboard a train were neither cheap nor palatable in his experience, and given a choice in the matter he would rather sit to table in the greasiest trackside café than in the finest dining car.

He had not gone a hundred yards when a sound to his rear turned his stomach cold.

The hollow bark of a revolver reached him on the street, then twice more.

Longarm dropped both his McClellan and valise and whirled, his hand instinctively snaking the Colt out of its holster as he turned.

As if the gunshots had been a cue, a rider bolted out of an alley farther down the street and raced forward leading a string of four saddled and riderless horses.

The rider came to a hoof-sliding halt immediately in front of the marshal's office, and the led horses piled up in a whinnying, head-tossing jumble behind him.

Half a hundred to one, Longarm thought, that well-dressed rider's name was Calder. And that was his damned brother inside the jail.

The range was more than eighty yards between Calder and where Longarm stood, much too long for a handgun,

15

and a running man can't shoot worth dried shucks. Besides, it takes some time to get a cell door open, especially if the man with the key is in a hurry.

Longarm knelt and pulled his Winchester from the boot strapped to his saddle. There was already a cartridge in the chamber so he thumbed back the hammer and, still kneeling as if he were on a firing range, took careful aim toward the man he assumed was Calder.

With a rifle the mounted man was a dead-certain target at this distance. Literally dead. Any time Longarm chose to press the trigger.

But, damnit, he was only *assuming* that this was a jail-break and that the man sitting down there was one of the Calders. He did not truly *know* that it was so.

It was possible—damned unlikely, but certainly within the realm of possibility—that this man and the one inside were just high-spirited good citizens in a big hurry to tell young Perk some happy news.

After all, Longarm hadn't actually *seen* the gunshots fired. He could not know with absolute certainty that those shots had come from inside the jail.

Longarm groaned. He held his point of aim. But he also held his fire.

The man on the horse saw him now, down the street, kneeling, aiming a rifle. The man—it just *had* to be Calder—reacted by pulling his revolver and aiming it toward Longarm.

Still the deputy had to keep his rifle silent. Longarm was not wearing a badge. If this guy on the horse was—fat chance—some innocent citizen, he could not know who Longarm was or what he was up to. And anybody with all his senses had the right to return fire when some stranger shot at him or was about to. Longarm gritted his teeth and kept his finger off the trigger.

The man fired, but at that range the bullet went so wide that Longarm never even heard it pass. He hoped no one behind him came to harm from it.

16

The door of the jail swung open, and four men came rushing into the street. One of them was the well dressed man Longarm had nodded to when they passed on the sidewalk moments before. The other three Longarm had last seen on the far side of a set of bars.

All right, then, Longarm thought. That was more than enough proof of what was going on.

He applied the last ounce of pressure needed to trip the sear blocking the Winchester's hammer, and the rifle bellowed and jolted back against his shoulder. The mounted Calder swayed in his saddle, dropped his revolver, and pitched face forward into the hard-packed dirt of the Cheyenne street. From the sickeningly unprotected way he fell, Longarm knew he was already dead before he hit the ground.

When Calder fell he also released his grip on the reins of the horses he had been leading, and the excitement of the running men and the gunshots already had the animals nervous. As soon as they were free they spun and bolted down the street, leaving the remaining four men afoot.

The remaining Calder brother was armed, and at least one of the sprung prisoners had grabbed a weapon on his way out. They snapped shots in Longarm's direction and scuttled back toward the jail.

In an Eastern city they might well have gotten away with it, at least to the point of being able to barricade themselves in the jail and making a siege of it. But Cheyenne was no Eastern city, and its menfolk did not necessarily expect some hired patrolman with a blue suit and brass buttons to protect them. The men of Cheyenne went armed and were as often as not fully capable of protecting themselves.

Once the jailbreak was discovered and the shots fired, most of the men who were near pulled their guns and joined in.

Longarm's fire was only part of a fusillade that tore at the front of the marshal's office and into the bodies of the fleeing felons.

Only one of the Calder gang lived to reach the doorway,

17

and he was dragging one leg and bleeding profusely when he disappeared from sight.

The townsmen, a rapidly growing number of them, continued to rain bullets through the open doorway and now glassless windows of the marshal's office.

"Hold your fire. Damn it, boys, hold it!" Longarm shouted and waved his arms as he stepped into the street. Gradually the gunfire diminished and finally stopped.

"I'm a deputy United States marshal, boys, so go easy here." He had been more than half worried that some excited son would go trigger-happy and shoot him too when he tried to calm them down. He waited a moment to let that information sink in, then pulled his badge and showed it to the men who were peering out of the doorways and from behind parked wagons up and down the length of the block. "Easy now."

He pointed to the nearest group of men, half a dozen of them with revolvers and one man with a shotgun. "You boys cover me. The rest of you hold your fire. I'm going to go see of we still have a fight here, or if it's all over." He waited until he got some nods of acknowledgement before he walked cautiously forward with the Winchester trailed in his left hand and the Colt ready now in his right.

He stooped low to go in front of the jail window and reached the doorway without incident. He was frankly more worried about the men on the street than he was about the single wounded robber who might be holed up inside, but no one shot.

"We're ready, Marshal," someone called out.

Longarm nodded. He hoped they weren't too damned ready. It really would be discouraging to be shot in the back by someone who was supposed to be on the same side of this scrap.

He waited for a moment, listening, but he could hear nothing from inside the jail.

The sporting thing to do, he guessed, would be to an-

18

nounce his intention of going in. But then this wasn't his idea of sport.

Moving with a fluid, catlike speed, Longarm crouched and launched himself through the doorway. He landed on his shoulder, rolled, and stopped belly down on the floor with the Colt at the ready.

"Aw . . . shit." He got to his feet, shoved the .44-40 back into its holster, and began to brush the dirt off his clothes.

The last member of the Calder gang was dead.

So was young Perk.

Calder had shot him in the face. His body lay behind Kyle Lewis's desk, legs entangled in the overturned swivel chair. His revolver was still in its pouch on his belt.

Longarm looked at the young deputy and grieved for him.

More than grief, though, Longarm wished there was some way he could apologize to the kid.

"You had good reason to be fretful, boy," he told the dead deputy. "If I said anything to make you less cautious . . ." He could not finish the thought. Not aloud, anyway.

He turned back toward the men who would still be poised outside waiting to pour gunfire into the jail. There was a lot of cleaning up to do here, and a lot of paperwork would have to be filled out. By somebody.

Longarm hoped Lewis had another deputy in town who could handle that chore. He truly did not want to have to stay around and face Kyle Lewis when he got back from Torrington.

Chapter 3

By the time he reached Reno, the little tank town at the foot of the Sierras that used to be known as Truckee Meadows, Longarm was already more than half a day behind the schedule he had set for himself.

His sense of urgency no longer had anything to do with Brenda Savoit. That intended dalliance no longer had much interest for him. Not that Longarm was thinking about giving up sex. It was just that finding the Professor was so damned important. And the end of the month was approaching all too quickly. He had less than two weeks left, if the informant's information had been correct.

Once old T. Anthony had his stake he would be gone, far away from the U.S.A., and he was more than bright enough to be able to lose himself, quite comfortably and happily, on another continent, damn him.

In addition to the sense of simple duty that always prompted Custis Long to give his best to the badge he wore, there was a personal consideration involved here too, something that had nothing to do with the Professor but much to do with Longarm's sense of self-worth. He was still feeling responsible for the death in Cheyenne of city deputy Alfred Ray Perkins III. He needed this arrest, not for absolution — nothing would ever really give him that — but for a small measure of assurance that he could be trusted to handle the damned job.

Perkins's death had shaken him, even though he was not technically or legally liable. Oh, there had been no trouble about it back in Cheyenne. No one had made any accusations or pointed any fingers. Kyle Lewis's chief deputy took Longarm's statement and collected statements as well from a dozen or more townspeople. There would be no charges or inquest appearances.

Custis Long was not so easy on himself.

All through the night, when he finally was able to board a westbound coach, he fretted and worried about the advice he had given that young deputy.

For himself that advice would not have been wrong. Longarm knew how to handle himself, knew how to read a nicely dressed, seemingly respectable stranger coming through an office door.

His error had been in giving advice to a youngster who was not mature enough, did not have the nerve and the judgment to be able to use that advice correctly.

And now, now that Longarm understood his error, it was just too damned late for the knowledge to do young Perk any good.

In Ogden, waiting for the changeover train from the Union Pacific tracks to the Western line, he ordered a meal and found the food tasted like so much dust in his mouth.

Even a belt of good Maryland rye, found only after diligent search and at an exorbitant price in that predominantly Mormon, very nearly dry city, had failed to revive his tastebuds. The rye could have been so much lukewarm tea for all the satisfaction he got from it, so he shoved the remainder of the bottle into his bag and paced the depot platform while he waited for the next westbound passenger to be made up in the noisy yard.

21

Now, in Reno, Longarm was still fretful. But at least he was hungry again.

"How long to the next train down to Virginia City?" he asked the ticket man at the spur line's depot.

"Oh . . ." The man scratched his chin and looked up at a wall clock. "Three hours or so."

Longarm could have cursed. It was another delay—minor, to be sure—but it seemed to be just another indication of the way this job was going.

Still, there was no point in browbeating people who couldn't do anything to help a bad situation. Longarm could stand here for the entire three hours and cuss the clerk, but that would neither make him feel any better nor make the next train move any earlier. Longarm thanked the man, decided against lugging his gear with him this time, and deposited his bag and saddle with the baggage agent for the line. Not wanting to push temptation but so far, though, he carried his Winchester with him when he left to go in search of a restaurant.

There was not much to choose from. A ramshackle little dump near the depot, obviously there to serve railroading crews, had a sign out front offering eats and cots. Down the street there was a hotel with a tall false front hiding tired, rickety-looking timbers behind. As far as Longarm could see there was not much about the town to recommend it. He walked past the café and headed for the hotel.

"Afternoon," he said to the woman who seemed to be in charge of the hotel's tiny restaurant.

"Pick your spot," she said, and hurried off. Apparently she was doing all the work in the place, and most of the tables were filled. It was only half past noon, and the restaurant had a good trade for such a small town. Most of the men at the tables were dressed like drummers or some sort of businessmen. There seemed to be no cattlemen or cowboys among them, which reminded Longarm that he had come to a completely foreign section of the West, much

22

different from the country he was used to. Business here had to do with railroads and with minerals that could be taken out of the ground, not with anything that could be grown or raised on top of it.

He found an unoccupied table near the back wall and settled down to wait. It was beginning to look like he would need the entire three-hour layover just to have his lunch.

The hostess or waitress or whatever she might be carried food to one table, took orders at two others, and brought meals to another table before she finally had time to ask what Longarm wanted.

"Steak if it's handy, ma'am, and taters and coffee. That would fill the emptiness just fine."

She gave him a brief flicker of smile and hurried on to another table to take their order.

Longarm was feeling more relaxed now, and the sleep he had lost in the cinder- and smoke-filled passenger coaches getting here was starting to catch up with him. He rested his boots on the unused chair opposite him at the small table and lighted a cheroot to pass the time while he waited for his food.

After less time than he had really expected, the lady was back with a platter of steak and potatoes and biscuits. She had a bowl of dark gravy and a heavy crockery cup of ink-black coffee.

"That looks real nice, ma'am." Longarm eased his boots down to the floor and stubbed his cigar out in an ash-filled saucer that had been left on the table for that purpose. "Thank you."

Again she gave that brief but rather nice smile, and turned away.

"Hey, you!" a man at the next table yelled.

"Sir?" the waitress asked.

"Yeah, you, damnit. C'm'ere."

She looked annoyed, but only mildly so, as she stepped to the table. He was a big man, dressed in broadcloth and

23

with a bat-wing collar. He was sitting with two other gentle-men—or men dressed the way gentlemen were expected to—and all three of them looked angry.

"Where the hell do you get off serving him before us?" the angry customer demanded. He pointed an accusing fin-ger at Longarm.

"His order was placed first, sir. Now, if you'll excuse me?" She started to turn away.

"Hold on, damn it. Our order was put in first and you fed this man first. Now you get your butt into that kitchen and bring us our food *now*."

The harried woman blushed a bright red and would have hurried away from the table, but the man caught her wrist and held her there. "Did you hear me?" he thundered.

"I . . ."

"Fucking bitch. Move." He tossed her wrist away from him like he was trying to throw her toward the kitchen.

The language the man had been using before was bad enough and entirely too much. This last, though, was the final straw and then some.

Longarm left his steak untouched before him and stood up. He was beside the other table in two strides.

The waitress was still standing there. She was red-faced and crying and seemed too upset even to flee toward the safety of the kitchen.

Longarm gentled her with a touch on the shoulder and said, "It's going to be all right, ma'am. These gentlemen are going to apologize for their behavior." He turned toward the three men still sitting at the table and, with his eyes locked cold and deadly on the loudmouth, added, "Aren't you?"

The two who had been silent turned their heads away. It was obvious that they wanted no part of a fuss. One of them did mumble something that was probably intended to be an apology, and the other soon followed suit.

"Now you, sir," Longarm suggested in a deceptively gentle tone.

The man glared up at Longarm. "You're the..." His voice died away as he got a better look at the ice in Longarm's flashing eyes and the tall deputy's deadpan expression.

"What?" Longarm demanded.

The man paused for a moment, then seemed to get his courage back. "You're the son of a bitch that started all this."

Longarm smiled at him, but there was no humor at all in his smile. "Two suggestions, sir. One, keep your language suitable for a lady's ears. Two, tell me that again where there isn't a lady present."

"Son of a bitch," the man accused again.

"Ma'am, would you excuse us, please?" Longarm asked mildly. He motioned the waitress toward the kitchen, and after a moment's hesitation she went.

All the men in the hotel restaurant, Longarm noticed, had become silent. Their eyes followed the waitress out of sight and then returned rather eagerly to the table where the quiet dispute was going on.

If the dumb bastard with the big mouth had been willing to let it lie there, Longarm would have been willing to return to his table and finish his meal before the steak got cold. But the man was not that bright.

He stood and glared at Longarm. On his feet he was tall, at least as tall as Longarm, and built with more beef across his shoulders. He was much thicker in the body, but he looked like he was in good shape.

"Shouldn't we go outside where we won't be breaking things?" Longarm suggested.

"So you can run away easier?" the man sneered.

Longarm grinned at him. "Not hardly."

The man grunted and motioned for Longarm to lead the way.

Longarm started toward the front door. It was a mistake. Behind him the bastard slammed a clubbed fist into the small of Longarm's back, narrowly missing the intended

25

kidney area and sending the lean, muscular deputy stumbling forward in sudden, unexpected pain.

The man had already established the rules. Now it was Longarm's turn to play.

He caught himself before he fell and flung himself backward, spinning and swinging around with the edge of his hand as he turned.

He intended to chop the man in the throat and end the fight there and then, but the fellow was fast as well as dirty. He ducked and instead of landing in the soft flesh of the vulnerable throat the punch caught the man on the shelf of the jaw. The force of the blow was enough to spin him and split the skin, spraying blood over customers at another table nearby, but he was still very much in the fracas.

Longarm continued his spin and stopped facing the man. He raised his forearms as a guard and slipped several hard, fast punches that the fellow threw his way.

Longarm grinned at him. "You've fought in the ring."

"You damn well bet I have," the man said. As he was still speaking he threw a haymaker that would have knocked a horse silly, but Longarm sent it off target with a flick of his forearm.

If this had been official business, something in the line of duty, Longarm would have ended it the easy way, with his Colt. But this was a private matter. And the simple fact of being an asshole was not grounds for capital punishment. That was a good thing, Longarm had often thought, because if that ever became law it would decimate the population almost instantly.

Longarm ignored the cold steel Peacemaker on his belt and slipped inside the ex-boxer's guard to land a fast combination into the man's gut.

It was like hitting a plank of "soft" pine, and Longarm's hands stung, probably more than the man's belly did. Still, it did have the desired effect of bringing the man's guard down, and Longarm popped him flush on the face with a right. To protect his own hands, Longarm hit out with the butt of his palm, and the fellow's nose sprayed blood. Long-arm hoped none of it was getting on his tweed coat; blood-stains could be remarkably difficult to get rid of.

The ex-boxer roared with anger and forgot his training. He tried to rush Longarm, his arms windmilling wild punches, and Longarm backed away quickly, then sidestepped. As the man came forward, Longarm moved to the side. He tripped the fellow and clubbed him over the ear as he went down.

The man hit the floor with a look of amazement creeping through the blood coating his face. He hung on hands and knees, shaking his head and speckling the plank flooring with drops of bright scarlet. He reminded Longarm of a bull, tired and hurting and slinging slobbers before it goes down in the *corrida*.

"Now I see why you left the ring," Longarm said calmly.

The man reacted by bellowing his rage again and spinning on hands and knees to lunge upward with a slashing uppercut toward Longarm's groin.

"That's naughty," Longarm said, and kicked the man in the face.

Longarm's boot caught him under his jaw and flipped him over onto his back, where he lay for almost a minute shaking his head. His eyes were glassy.

"I think," Longarm said to the fellow's companions, "you really oughta haul this bastard out of here before somebody gets mad at him."

One of the others sighed and both of them stood. They looked so angry that for a moment Longarm thought he was going to have to fight them too.

Then they looked down at the fallen fighter, and Longarm could see that their disgust was directed toward that man and not toward himself.

"The thing is," one of them said, "the stupid slob *hadn't* left the ring. He was set for a fight down in Virginia City. Supposed to be his big comeback on the way to the title." The man made a face like he wanted to spit. "We're his

27

managers. *Were* his managers. You can have him now if you want him. I don't." He made a shoving motion with his hands, threw a fold of paper money onto the table to pay for the as-yet-undelivered meal, and walked out of the place. The other man followed him.

The fighter—former fighter now—sat up and watched them go. "I messed up, didn't I?" he asked miserably.

"Uh-huh."

The boxer came to his feet, and Longarm stood ready for another round with him, but the fellow was no longer interested. He used a napkin to wipe some of the blood from his face and sighed. "I don't suppose you know where a man could find work around here?"

"No, I'm just passing through."

"So was I—I thought." He picked up his hat and started to leave.

"Wait," Longarm said.

"Yeah?"

"You still owe the lady an apology."

The former boxer looked thoroughly cowed now. He flushed, but he did not try to fight any more.

Hat in hand, trying to ignore the sidelong glances from the other diners in the place, he made his way through the tables to the kitchen door. He opened it and spoke to someone inside, presumably the waitress who had been so offended by his language. After a moment he turned and shuffled out the front door. He reminded Longarm of a schoolboy caught trying to peek under the teacher's skirts and made to take his licking in front of the class.

Longarm returned to his meal, but he couldn't enjoy it. The damned steak was cold.

On the other hand, he got excellent service after that, and he got a distinct impression that if he got back this way and had enough time he would not have to spend his layover alone. It was just a pity that he did not have more time here between trains.

28

Chapter 4

The spur line ran south and east from Reno to reach the fabulous bonanza town of Virginia City. The tracks climbed and twisted into a series of abrupt hills that were completely unlike the Rocky Mountain country Longarm had just left.

Here the vegetation ran to saltbush and sage, the slopes dotted with stunty-looking piñons. There was practically nothing in sight that a man on horseback could not see over without having to stand in his stirrups.

It was arid, high desert country with too little graze to attract stockmen. Except for the lure of minerals it likely would have been innocent of humanity, Longarm thought. Certainly he saw nothing here to attract a person.

The majesty of the Sierras, lying tantalizingly close to the west, made the contrast between that timbered country and this barren land all the more apparent.

Still, Longarm had not come here to see the sights, but to do a job.

It was already dark before the overworked puffer reached a final downgrade and pulled into the depot at Virginia City for a hard-earned rest. Longarm's first impression of the

29

town was of a wall of lights rising above him to the west. The sharply rising hillside against which Virginia City was built showed an almost solid wall of lamp-lighted windows, and he did not need sunshine to tell him that there would be no tempting view of the far mountains from this town.

The city also seemed much larger than he had expected. He had no idea of the population as yet, but certainly this was no flash-in-the-pan boom town that would quickly blossom and as quickly fade. The Comstock had already been in operation for twenty years or so, and the area was still producing, the town still frantic in its activity.

Longarm stepped down from the single passenger car on the mixed freight and passenger train and hefted his gear. He asked directions to a decent but not fancy hotel and was sent a hard-climbing two blocks above the station to a place called the Buckhorn, although why it might be called that Longarm could not figure. Any self-respecting mulie would have to be plumb lost to wander into country like this.

He took a room at the exorbitant rate of two-fifty per night and had the good sense to sign a government voucher for his expenses there rather than promising cash payment at the end of his stay. Rates like that, he knew, could run a man out of expense money on the double quick.

His second-floor room—if they were going to stiff him for that kind of room rate he was not willing to climb all the way to the fourth floor for the privilege of being fleeced—was only average. But it did have a hasp on either side of the door and a sturdy padlock that could be applied inside or out, as the tenant required. Longarm took only a moment to dump his bag on the bed, stash his saddle in a handy corner, and lock the room up tight before he went back downstairs.

"Could you tell me where to find all the sights?" he asked the night clerk.

"The Crystal Palace is one block down. Piper's Op'ry House is on the same street. Whatever you want, just look for it; it'll be there day or night."

30

"By down you'd mean south?" Longarm asked.

The clerk gave him a pained look. "By down I'd mean 'down,' mister. Like in down the damned hill."

"Oh. Well . . . thank you."

The man grunted and went back to a book he was reading.

"Oh, one other thing," Longarm said.

"Yeah?"

"The sheriff's office." Virginia City was a county seat, and courtesy would require him to check in with the local law.

"That'd be in the courthouse. First floor. Out this door and turn left. You can't miss it."

"Thanks," Longarm said again.

He stepped out into the cool night air and paused to reset his Stetson. The country here did not look like the area he was used to, but it did feel the same. There was that same clean, healthy bite in the air when he stepped outside despite the sun heat that had been so strong during the day.

The courthouse—he was almost surprised, but it really was the kind of structure you couldn't miss—was a tall affair built of stone in a narrow-fronted style. At the moment it was also locked tight, and there was no sign of any lights on the first floor, where the sheriff's office was supposed to be.

Longarm thought he could stand the disappointment. If the local law was all that straight he would have thought the informant would have told them about it instead of traveling all the way to Cheyenne before he stopped to look up a lawman. So while Longarm was not going to the extreme of leaping to a conclusion about the locals he was at least going to be cautious in his dealings with them. Judgement could wait until all the facts were in.

He stopped before the darkened courthouse to light a cheroot and turned down the hill toward the raucously busy main street of the wide-awake town.

It was early evening, and the saloons certainly sounded full. Past experience with mining camps, though, told Long-

31

arm that it would have made no difference if he first hit the street in mid-morning or four A.M. Men working underground timed their lives by the shift whistle, not the sun, and took their relaxation at any time they were not swinging a pick or packing giant powder. To a miner the time of day—or the time of night—meant nothing.

Longarm reached the street level and turned south toward the busiest, best lighted business district. Storefront after storefront offered liquor, gaming, and women, in roughly that order of apparent importance.

His first surprise was when he stopped at the Crystal Palace in search of a drink.

No roughshod, sawdust-floored shanty this, but an opulently crafted, richly decorated, actually quite elegant house of relaxation. Longarm had to remind himself that he was not in some boom town here, but a solidly established city that worked at least as hard as it played.

The men taking their ease in the Palace this night were for the most part handsomely turned out in suits and ties and derby hats. The drillers and muckers apparently were expected to do their drinking in lesser establishments.

This, Longarm thought immediately, would be the ideal place to look for the Professor. As far as Longarm knew, no one had ever quite determined if Scott's nickname was earned or self-appointed, but he was a man who fancied himself as high-toned and preferred to pass himself off as a gentleman of quality.

The tall deputy crossed the floor to the bar, a gleamingly polished affair of dark wood with a brass rail below, and asked for Maryland rye.

"Yes, sir." No hesitation here, or any suggestion of a substitute. There were, after all, advantages to a moneyed environment.

Longarm paid for the drink and savored it while he looked over the crowd.

Most of the men were gathered at tables in small groups, drinking slowly while they talked. Longarm could overhear nearly all the conversations, and he made a conscious effort to listen in on as many as possible that were related to mining. Words like stope and drift and amalgam were prominent.

One side of the huge room was devoted to tables and wheels where a man could try his luck. The wheel of fortune was popular, as were faro and monte. The men who were gambling here used hard money only, and all of it gleamed yellow in the bright lamplight. Silver seemed to be something for pikers, even at the table where they were piking monte.

"Something else, mister?"

"What? Oh." Longarm smiled at the bartender and pushed his glass forward. "A refill."

The man poured it and collected a dime from the change Longarm had left on the bar.

"Thanks. Nice place you have here," Longarm said.

The barman grunted.

"Say, I'm looking for a friend of mine. You might've seen him here."

"I see a lot of people here."

"His name is Scott, Professor Scott, but he might be using another at the moment." Longarm winked at the fellow. "Woman trouble, if you know what I mean."

The bartender nodded seriously. It was not an unusual situation, and a man was free to take any name he wished when he reached a new town. In country like this people neither asked nor cared what a man's name or reputation had been in the past. It was what he did among his new neighbors that would count. "What's he look like, this friend of yours?"

"He . . ." Longarm stopped. What the hell *did* Scott look like now? "Average, I guess. Medium height, medium build. Maybe forty."

The barman tried to suppress a smile and was almost successful. "I expect I've seen a couple fellows I could call average lately. Could be one of them was your friend."

33

Longarm grinned. "Sorry about that."

The bartender laughed with him. "Look, I don't recall anybody named Scott, but if I do meet up with somebody of that name I could tell him you're looking for him, Mr. . . . uh . . ."

"I guess maybe that could be awkward, come to think of it. He might not want to see me just now." Longarm reached into his coat pocket for his wallet and flipped it open.

"Woman trouble don't normally get that serious, Marshal."

"Yeah, well . . ."

"Not that it's any of my never mind, of course."

"Thanks."

"Look, I got nothing against the law, Marshal. So if I do meet up with your friend, well, I reckon I could tell you about it."

"There could be a reward in it for you."

The man looked skeptical, so Longarm added, "Federal officers aren't allowed to collect reward bounties."

The bartender grinned. "A friend of mine a while back, he was told the same thing by . . . well, the name don't matter. By a local badge, it was, anyway. This friend went out of his way to help. Put the finger on a fella with a hundred dollars on his head and turned him in to this here local deputy. The deputy tells him the reward's been withdrawn. Then a week or so later the deputy turns up with a new suit of clothes and a diamond stickpin in his tie. Makes a body wonder, that does."

Longarm nodded. "You can check out what I told you. You can also have my word on it."

The man looked at him closely. Then he smiled. "I guess I'll settle for your word, Marshal." He reached across the bar to shake. "Jacobs is the name. Everybody calls me Jake."

"Long. They call me Longarm."

"Now I wonder why that would be so, Longarm?"

Longarm sighed and shook his head. "I never have figured that one." He grinned and bought another drink for himself and one for Jake Jacobs.

He spent the next several hours idling in the Palace and in several others of the many saloons and gambling houses in Virginia City, but he saw nothing of the Professor nor of the one-legged man known as Duck. They would be the two easiest to identify of the Professor's alleged robbery gang, but he neither saw nor heard anything about them. Eventually he gave it up as wasted effort and climbed back uphill to the Buckhorn Hotel.

He had started the night with the Maryland rye and finished it with beer in the less well stocked saloons where he had hoped for a line on Duck Bragg, but he had not yet taken time for a meal since he'd arrived.

The hotel restaurant was nearly empty when he got there, and most of the lamps had already been extinguished.

"Am I too late to get a bite?" he asked the man who was stacking chairs upside down on the table tops and getting ready to mop the floor.

The fellow grunted.

Longarm was about to turn away, resigned to choosing between a supperless night or another walk down the steep hillside, when he heard the light sound of footsteps behind him.

"Surely it isn't too late, is it?"

It was a woman's voice, and Longarm had some idea of her looks before he ever turned to see. The swamper in the restaurant had not been at all eager to reopen the place for a male customer, but now he was looking suddenly shy and pleased and was already taking chairs back down from a table near the kitchen door. "No'm," the man said, "no trouble at all, an' you ain't too late by a single minit."

Longarm looked.

No wonder the swamper had reacted that way.

35

The girl—she looked to be scarcely more than that—was worth some extra trouble just for the privilege of being able to look at her.

She was small, five feet give or take an inch, but she had a figure that could only be considered lush. She had dark hair pinned high under a jaunty hat of dark green velvet. The hat reminded Longarm of an illustration he had seen once in a book about an English bandit named Robin Hood. Longarm had not really enjoyed the book; he kept finding his sympathies on the wrong side of the game and kept wondering why people always wanted to glorify dashing crooks, regardless of their motives. But this girl's hat went very well with the pretty but determined look she wore.

She had on a dark green dress and cloak to match the hat, or perhaps it was the other way around. Longarm guessed she was in her early twenties. She was carrying a green velvet handbag and a leather folio.

Longarm swept his Stetson off and stood aside for her to enter the dining room before him.

"Thank you, sir."

"Yes, ma'am."

She pouted. "Miss, if you please, sir."

"As you wish, miss."

"A table, please?" she asked the swamper.

"Yes'm." The poor man nearly tripped over his own feet getting a chair into position for her.

"And you, sir, will you be eating also?" she asked Longarm.

"I expect to, if they're willing to cook for two."

"Then join me, please, if you would not mind company."

"I'd be pleased, miss." Longarm helped himself to a chair across the table from the girl. He was aware of a rather jealous look from the swamper-turned-waiter.

"Tell me about yourself," the girl ordered. As she spoke she unstrapped her folio and opened it to disclose a pad of paper and a box of lead pencils. She smiled very sweetly.

36

Chapter 5

"You, uh, wouldn't mind if I asked what you're doing there, would you?" Longarm asked the girl.

"Of course not," she said briskly. "I intend to take notes on what you say. A man's life and exciting times in a mining camp. You know."

"Maybe I don't," Longarm said. "Why?"

"I am a journalist, sir." The girl managed to look prim and slightly smug about her announcement. "Name, please?"

"Custis Long." The nearly blunt tip of her pencil scratched across the paper.

The girl looked up and gave him a look that she probably intended to be shrewdly searching. To Longarm it looked more like she was squinting in bad light. With no small degree of effort, he was able to keep a straight face.

"Mining engineer?" she suggested.

"No, ma'am. Excuse me," he hastily corrected, *"miss."*

"Are you—"

"You haven't told me your name yet," he interrupted.

She looked mildly annoyed, but after the briefest moment

she flashed him a smile instead of a scowl. "Millicent Cater," she said.

"Called Milly?"

"Called Miss Cater, normally. Are you—"

"Are you really a journalist?"

Millicent Cater flushed slightly, and Longarm suspected he had unknowingly hit on a sore point. She was not so easily put on the defensive, though. "Have you any reason to believe I am not, Mr. Long?"

"None at all," Longarm assured her. "You seem quite competent. What newspaper do you represent?"

She flushed again, more obviously this time. "That seems beside the point, Mr. Long."

"Not at all, Miss Cater. A gentleman should always be careful where and how his name will be used."

This time Millicent did look definitely annoyed. She solved the problem by motioning for the waiter/swamper to come take their order.

The man seemed more than willing to approach the pretty girl at the table. He was beside them within seconds. There were, Longarm thought, certain benefits to being seen in the company of beauty.

"There ain't much but simple stuff available this time o' night," the waiter said. "You'd best make it easy."

The girl put on a thoughtful expression and in an aside to Longarm said, "Don't you simply love the local foods here? Beans, for instance. I would really adore a bowl of beans this evening." She smiled up at the waiter.

Sure she wanted beans, Longarm thought. Loved the damn soggy things, no doubt. It wouldn't have anything to do with the fact that beans were cheap. Which might also explain her reluctance to name the newspaper she was supposed to be working for.

"A steak for me," Longarm said. "Fried in tallow. And fried potatoes too." To the girl he added, "Begging your pardon, Miss Cater, but if you haven't tried steak the way the cattlemen like it, it would be my pleasure to introduce you to it. My treat, so to speak." He smiled.

"Are you sure, Mr. Long?"

"You really should give it a try," he urged.

"If you insist."

"Do that twice then," Longarm told the waiter. "And a coffee and...?" He looked at the girl.

"Tea, please."

"If we got any." The waiter shuffled off to deliver their order to the kitchen.

"That is very kind of you, Mr. Long."

"My pleasure, Miss Cater. You never told me just which paper it is you're working for."

"Oh, I'm from back East," the girl said airily.

"Big place, I'm told."

"What is?"

"East." He smiled. "From here that kinda takes in most of the country."

"I suppose it does." She began fiddling with the napery that had been left on their table.

Longarm said gently, "You aren't exactly employed by a newspaper at the moment, are you." It was not really a question.

Millicent's face crumpled, and Longarm thought she was going to cry. He was relieved when she did not. "It's...it's...*unfair,* that's what it is."

"Tell me about it."

A sympathetic ear was all that was needed to loosen the floodgates of her frustration.

She was from Buffalo—Longarm did not even need to ask which Buffalo, Wyoming or Texas or whatever; it seemed only too obvious that it was the misnamed city in New York State that she was talking about—and she just *knew* she had what it took to become a truly discerning journalist and a reporter of great impact. It was just those damn fool, hidebound editors, all of them *men,* who were holding her back.

But she *knew* she could do the job. If only they would

let her. They just didn't *want* a woman to prove herself. She was convinced of that.

Well, Millicent Cater was going to show them. She was going to be so damned good that they would *have* to hire her. Her jaw was set and her eyes—brilliant green, almost matching her dress and hat, Longarm noticed now, and lightly flecked with gold—were flashing when she got around to that part.

"I came out here to Virginia City because the *Territorial Enterprise* here is supposed to be the very best small newspaper there is anywhere. Sam Clemens used to write for the *Enterprise,* and Bret Harte." That seemed to mean a great deal to her although Longarm had only a great deal to her although Longarm had only vaguely heard of either of them. "And I thought that maybe here they would be willing to judge quality before gender." The lively animation that had been in her expression faded. "I was wrong," she finished miserably.

"I see."

Millicent gave him a worried look. "I suppose you are like all the rest. You think I should give up and go back home, too."

"I think," Longarm said, "that you are a very determined young woman. If pure grit will get the job done, then I think you can do it and do it well."

She brightened.

"On the other hand," Longarm added, "I don't run any newspapers, and I'm not in any position to give you a job." He smiled and reached forward to pat the back of her wrist. "I would if I could, Miss Cater."

"Thank you, Mr. Long. And you may call me Millicent if you prefer."

"My friends call me Longarm."

"Really? Why?"

He shrugged. "Just a nickname I picked up along the line." His instincts told him that, while he did not actually want to lie to this girl, he likely would be much better off

40

if she did not learn that he was a deputy United States marshal. To an Eastern girl with journalistic ambitions that would sound entirely too romantic and dangerous and exciting and, worst of all, potentially newsworthy for his future comfort. If he could avoid any repeats of her early line of questioning he certainly intended to do so.

The waiter saved him this time, returning with a tray held awkwardly low. The meal, Longarm noted with satisfaction, looked to be much better than the service.

Millicent tore into the meat and potatoes with no sign of feminine, bird-picking pretense. Longarm wondered just how long she had been living on the cheap. Not that it was any of his business, of course.

When the virtually silent meal was done he asked, "Would you care for anything else?"

She looked at him and hesitated for a moment, then said, "There is one thing."

"Yes?"

"I...uh...am not registered at the hotel."

"No?"

"I had been staying at a...well, to be polite about it, I should have to call it a lesser establishment than this."

"So?"

She sighed. "So I seem to have been locked out of my room. Actually."

The obvious solution would have been for Longarm to offer her a "loan." But, aside from his normal reluctance to have anyone put the touch on him, he had brought practically no money of his own that he would be free to hand out. It hardly seemed ethical to shovel out taxpayer's funds from his expense money so some would-be newspaper reporter could pay a board bill.

The next best thing was just as obvious. But he hoped the damned girl would neither misunderstand the offer nor interfere with the work he had come here to do. He cleared his throat.

"I suppose you could use my room," he said, quickly

adding, "There's a chair I could use for the night."

The girl brightened. "Thank you, Custis." She had no hesitation at all about accepting the offer. If he hadn't already been convinced that this girl was determined to succeed, he would have been now.

He paid their bill—Billy Vail wouldn't have to know exactly what a steak cost in Virginia City these days, and besides, maybe the girl would turn out to be a source of information, fat though that chance seemed—and led Miss Cater toward his room.

"What does your family think of your adventure?" he asked to make small talk on the way.

Millicent made a face. "Somewhat less than those pigheaded editors think of it," she admitted.

"No help there, huh?"

"None."

"Have you considered giving up?"

"Never," she said defiantly. She gave him a look of annoyance. "I thought you were on my side."

Longarm gentled her with a quick, "It was a question, Millicent, not a suggestion."

She gave him a grumpy harrumph, but seemed to be at least partially mollified.

Longarm unlocked the door to his room and stood aside for her to enter. He closed the door behind them and relocked it. When he saw the girl's eyes widen with uncertainty he smiled and said, "The lock is to keep people out, not in. You can have the key if you like. Better yet..." He used the key to unlock the sturdy padlock and let it dangle free in the hasp. No one could reach it from the outside to gain entry, but if the girl wanted to leave, she could do so.

Millicent smiled at him. "Thank you."

Longarm took his valise off the bed and dropped it in the corner next to his saddle. This was not, he thought, going to be exactly the kind of night's rest he had envisioned and had been looking forward to after a night and day on the rails.

42

He also stared long and hard at the single, straight-backed wooden chair that was provided for occupants of the rented room. Sleeping in that would be worse than trying to sleep on the train.

Millicent perched on the edge of the bed and watched while he unstrapped his bedroll from behind the cantle of his McClellan saddle and spread it on the floor at the foot of the bed.

"You are a man of your word, aren't you, Custis?"

"I do try." He arranged things to his liking, more or less, and removed his coat and vest and string tie, but he went no further than that. He pulled his boots off and set them beside his bedroll, then unbuckled his gunbelt and arranged it so that the grip of the Colt would be beside his head during the night.

"If you like," he said, "you can put the lamp out after I'm settled, and make yourself comfortable. I won't look."

"Truly?"

He smiled. "I didn't claim not to be tempted, but I reckon I'm grown enough to keep my eyes shut when I say I will." He knelt and crawled under the soogan that he had come to prefer to the scratchy warmth of Army-issue wool blankets.

From floor level the tall bulk of the bed would have kept him from seeing Miss Cater anyway, but he had said he would close his eyes, and close them he did. He could hear her leave the bed and move around a little, and after a moment the lamplight that was shining against his eyelids was extinguished. He could hear a good bit of cloth rustling against cloth as the girl removed at least some of her garments. A few moments more and he heard the faint protest of overused springs as she got into the bed.

"Good night, Custis."

"Good night, Millicent."

Longarm came to his knees with a hoarse croak of surprise caught in his throat. The Colt was in his hand without

conscious direction, and his finger was taut against the double-action trigger, the hammer already beginning to rise
from the slight pressure applied.

He heard a high-pitched, girlish squeak, and remembered
where and with whom he was. His finger went slack and a
lungful of tightly held breath was released with a rush.
"Damn, girl, you shouldn't ought to do that."

"I just . . . I'm sorry." He heard the scrape of a match
and the rattle of the lamp globe being lifted. Yellow light
flooded the room.

Millicent was wearing a chemise and her petticoats.
Longarm found it difficult to turn his eyes away from her.
Her figure was even more appealing with so little covering
it.

He turned his head and spent some unnecessary time
getting the Colt resituated in its holster on the floor. "I'm
sorry if I scared you," he said toward the roll of clean
clothing he was using for a pillow.

"I never thought . . . Custis?"

"Yes?"

"You never told me about yourself."

"No," he agreed.

"Are you a desperado?"

"No."

"Look at me, please."

He did. He liked what he saw. Perhaps too much.

"Tell me that again."

"I'm not a desperado, Millicent. I'll do you no harm."

Her face softened into a smile. "I believe you. Thank
you, Custis."

He nodded. "Are you all right?"

"I just couldn't sleep. I'm sorry I disturbed you." She
giggled. "Sorrier than you know. I was frightened for a
moment there."

"A man learns to be careful in strange rooms," he said.
"It wouldn't hurt you to learn the same."

"I'll try to remember that." She tilted her head to the

44

side and looked at him again, this time with a different kind of interest showing in her eyes. Longarm noticed that now, without the emerald of the hat and cloak so near, her eyes seemed more gold than green.

"You must think me a terribly brazen person, Custis."

"I think you're a very nice person, Millicent."

"I've . . . been alone for a very long time now."

"I suspect you've been frightened for longer than you want people to know, too," he said.

The girl dropped her eyes from his and looked down toward her hands. Her hands were very small. They were clutched in her lap as she sat on the edge of the rumpled bed. "I am not a virgin, Custis."

"Your business."

"I . . . would you please hold me?"

"I couldn't promise you it would stop there. You're a mighty pretty girl, Millicent."

She looked back toward him and smiled. "Thank you."

"Do you still want company?"

She licked her lips. And nodded.

Longarm should have felt tired. It was the middle of the night, and he had had little sleep since the long, boring train trip. Instead he felt very much rested and at ease.

Millicent Cater nestled against the hollow of his shoulder. Her eyelids drooped and fluttered open, drooped again and fluttered.

"You should try to get some rest now," he said.

She stirred and nipped at his chest with moist lips. "This is too delicious to let go."

"We have lots of time." He wanted a cigar but he did not want to disturb her.

He looked down at the girl with an expression that was softened by a newfound and genuine liking for her.

She was young and frightened and determined and honest, and he liked the things he was still learning about her.

She had been telling the truth when she said she was not

45

a virgin, but he suspected that her previous experience had been very, very limited. She had not been knowledgeable in the ways to please a man. But she had willingly learned a great deal in the past hour or so. And she had responded with unfeigned joy when he showed her the ways a man could please a woman. It had all seemed so new to her that he was certain her past experiences—or experience in the singular, which seemed more likely—had been less than enjoyable for her.

Millicent rolled slightly to the side and arched her back. "Kiss me again, Custis."

He bent to her and tasted her mouth. Her breath was sweet and her lips trembled.

"Thank you." She placed her fingertips against his temple and guided his head lower, positioning his lips over her breast. "Would you mind?"

He chuckled. "That, dear Milly, is a very foolish question."

Her breasts were large for a girl her size and had the taut, ripe fullness of youth. Her nipples were small and lightly pink. They were also very sensitive. He rolled his tongue around one, and Millicent groaned softly. He heard a sharp intake of breath when he drew one into his mouth and gently nipped it with his teeth.

Longarm had no right to get another erection so soon again, but obviously he was not as expert on that subject as he had thought he was.

Millicent apparently could feel the mindless, yearning flesh throbbing against her hip, because she reached down between them to fondle and caress him.

"Now, Custis. Please."

He raised himself over her, and she drew him deep into the warmth that was eagerly awaiting him. Millicent sighed happily.

Slowly, very slowly, Longarm began to move within her. She lay for a time, accepting him, then she began to move in rhythm with his long, slow, deep strokes.

46

Her hips rose and fell, and the faint creaking of the bedsprings was overcome with the much more interesting sound of flesh meeting flesh and the muted liquid noises as he pulled free of the wet grasp of her body at the end of each stroke.

Millicent's arms tightened around him, and he could feel the press of her nails digging into the hard muscles of his back. Her breath whistled in and out through clenched teeth, and he began to speed his motion to meet her rising needs.

She began to toss her head from side to side, and her small body bucked and shuddered beneath him.

She moaned and grabbed him with a final, belly-pounding convulsion as she tipped over the edge into ecstasy.

Her eyes were squeezed shut. After a moment she relaxed her hold on him and looked at him. There was happiness in her expression, and concern.

"You didn't, did you?"

He shook his head and smiled.

"This time."

She cupped his face in her small hands and raised her head so she could kiss him. "Promise?"

"Uh-huh."

"Good."

He was still socketed deep within her. Millicent began to move beneath him. When Longarm began to stroke with her she stopped him with a fingertip placed lightly against his lips.

"Let me this time. I think I can, you know."

Longarm grinned at her. "Personally, I'm plumb sure you can. An' dang near have already."

He could already feel the hot, good flow of building release gathering somewhere deep in his groin. Gathering strength and power for a final surge.

He held himself still and let her have the pleasure of bringing him to completion by her own swiftly learning efforts.

It was, after all, the polite thing to do for a lady.

His neck corded and his head arched backward as the first twinges of a gathering flow became a rushing torrent and as quickly an explosion.

He collapsed on top of her and only after several moments had passed was he aware that Millicent was cradling him to her, crooning, "Sleep now, sleep, my darling," in a soft whisper.

Longarm let his eyes sag shut and, still locked together, they drifted away into the deep sleep of satiation.

Chapter 6

Even after buying the girl a good breakfast and tactfully suggesting that she go off in search of a good story some-where—elsewhere—Longarm could not disengage himself from Millicent. She was deaf to his subtle suggestions and seemed determined to stick with him for the entire day, which was not exactly the way he had planned things.

The truth, he realized, was that she simply had nowhere else to go and nothing else to do. Damnit!

Professional courtesy required that he check in with the local law since he was now acting within their jurisdiction, but he really did *not* want a determined young female would-be reporter tailing him while he tried to conduct an inves-tigation. The mere thought of it raised visions of the lurid dime novels so popular back East.

Not that he had any remote objection to the idea of Millicent Cater being able to earn a living by writing im-aginatively inaccurate crap. He could not have cared less about that.

But, dammit, an appearance in one of those fool things was guaranteed to do two things. One, the lesser of the two, would be to make one Custis Long the laughingstock of the Denver Judicial District's deputy-U. S. marshals. That, though, he could live with if he had to.

The other, of much greater and more immediate concern, would be that having a damned girl reporter, however pretty she might be, tagging along in his footsteps would just as surely guarantee that he could accomplish not a damned thing here in Virginia City.

The Professor was a wary enough and bright enough man without adding the extra burden of drawing attention to Longarm with Millicent Cater's good looks and highly visible presence.

If Longarm intended to find the Professor and his gang— and he damn sure did have that intention—he was going to have to do it by slipping up on the crowd's blind side and spotting the Professor before he himself was sighted. He was hardly likely to do that if he went around the city with an entourage of reporters jabbering in his wake.

He sighed and tried to think of a way out while they finished their last cups of coffee after breakfast. Tea seemed a bit much even for Millicent at the early hour.

There was, Longarm reflected, at least one temporary benefit to having the girl so attached to him.

He knew full well that he had to see the sheriff here, and he was dreading the necessity.

The more he thought about the situation here, the more he kept coming back to the plain but as yet unexplained fact that the informant who had refused to be recruited by the gang had fled all the way to Cheyenne before he stopped and tipped the law to the deal.

The man might or might not have known he was being followed with murder in mind. That could explain, at least partially, why he ran so far.

But the odds were against it.

A clean, quiet knifing in a public place was not the sort of thing that was likely to happen when a man knew he was a target. A man who expected to be murdered might well

50

be taken in a public place. A crowded railway station was exactly the kind of place where a potential victim would try to hide himself.

But *quietly?* Longarm did not think so. A man attuned to that kind of wary readiness would be too quick to jump for that to seem likely.

So the odds, still quite unproven, favored the idea that the informant did not know he was targeted for murder. He *probably* thought he was making a clean break from the gang.

Longarm sighed.

That came right back to the original question. Why had the fellow run so far before he turned in a report to Kyle Lewis?

Rail connections might explain the distance involved, all the way from Virginia City in Nevada to Cheyenne in Wyoming Territory. Longarm had had to look at the train schedules for his own use earlier, and he knew that someone leaving Virginia City in the small hours of the morning would have to hustle to make all the connections if he wanted to run toward the east. So that might explain why this Mal, or Mel, had waited for the Cheyenne layover instead of making his report in Reno or Ogden. That would seem logical.

But why the hell would the man not have said anything to the law here in Virginia City?

Regardless of any train schedules, an informant passing information here could have gotten official protection from the law until he was well away from the scene.

Unless the local law was a party to the planned crime.

That, Longarm thought, was all too possible, given the other meager facts of this case.

So he was not entirely displeased that Millicent provided him with an excuse to delay his check-in with the local sheriff. The delay would give him a chance to do some looking around before any of the local badge-wearers knew there was a federal officer operating within their territory.

And if anyone questioned him about the lapse afterward he could quite honestly explain it away with Millicent's big-eared presence.

Things could have been better, Longarm thought, but they could as easily have been worse. He waited for Millicent to gather her handbag and folio ready to leave and wadded his own napkin on top of his quite thoroughly cleaned plate.

"Ready?"

She nodded.

He helped her with her chair and paid their bill, thinking as he did so that Billy Vail was certainly going to get a poor opinion of food prices in Virginia City. Still, it was all in the line of duty, more or less. He let Millicent take his arm and they left the Buckhorn for the bright sun glare of the city streets.

In daylight Virginia City was an impressive town in the midst of unimpressive country.

As he had expected from the pattern of the lighted windows the night before, there was no view from here of the majestic Sierras, but the city's buildings seemed to be constructed with an eye toward permanence and even in many cases elegance. Many of the major buildings were constructed of stone and some few were built of brick. There were few false fronts here and as far as he could see virtually no canvas structures concealed behind wooden street-front exteriors. In a mining town that was hardly the norm, and Longarm was impressed.

The countryside surrounding the city, though, was something else again. Drab and dry and barren, it was a study in the dull, muted colors of earth and broken rock.

The only green to be seen here was that which was painted on the buildings and the signs of the city, for there was not a single leaf or juniper needle within Longarm's range of vision.

That was common enough in the immediate vicinity of any mining camp. Every stick of wood within walking dis-

52

tance was likely to be stripped away for firewood or, if large enough, for shoring timbers inside the mine shafts.

But here that impression of desolation ran far into the distance as well.

Rolling, slightly lower country stretched away to the east from the hillside where the city was built, and even there and on the low hills to the east—the locals almost certainly would refer to the hills as mountains—there was practically no vegetation to be seen.

Dark shapes on the distant hillsides might have been piñon or juniper growth, but they might as easily have been dark rock formations jutting out through the stony soil. From so many miles away it was impossible to tell. This country could not compete with Longarm's home territory for natural beauty, he thought.

Still, he had not come here to be entertained by nature's glories. He had come here to do a job. The question now was how he was to go about that with Millicent Cater at his elbow.

"What did you have planned for the day?" he asked. He was quite frankly hoping she would give him an answer, *any* answer, that would give him an excuse to disengage himself from her for a while.

"Nothing, really." She gave his arm an affectionate squeeze and tilted her head back, rather far back from her short stature, to smile at him with her glowing green eyes. "I'd just like to walk around with you today, Custis."

"You don't have *any*thing in mind?"

"Oh, whatever I see or hear might be the basis for a good story. You can't plan those things, you know. So I'll be quite happy just being with you today. But I promise I'll be quiet as a little mouse and I won't get in your way, not the teeniest little bit." She smiled and hugged his arm.

Longarm fought down a case of the grumps he felt coming on. Quiet as a mouse, eh? Well, he could believe that, anyhow. Mice were noisy little bastards despite their reputations to the contrary.

53

She had already given him his excuse for not seeing the sheriff, and there was no point in carrying the matter to uncomfortable extremes. In a burst of inspiration that he thought would ditch her for sure he said, "I intend to spend some time in the saloons today, Millicent."

It was no secret that ladies did not frequent saloons. You might see a woman or two in some of the lower-class places, but none of them could be considered ladies by any charitable stretch of the imagination.

Longarm was quite sure that at the very worst Millicent would have to agree to meet him somewhere later, say for lunch.

Instead the damned girl squealed with delight—she was keeping her promise to be mouse-like, all right—and said, "But that's wonderful, Custis. You can't know how happy that makes me. I've been wanting some way to see inside those mysterious men-only haunts ever since I got here. And now that I have a proper escort, why, it couldn't be better."

The girl was grinning like a fool. But Longarm knew better. *He* was the fool of the moment. He felt like it anyhow.

Now that he had put his foot so firmly into the cow patty, he was just going to have to grin and wear it. He smiled back at her and led the way down toward the lower, and main, street level with Millicent clinging to his arm.

He looked at the Crystal Palace, thinking it would certainly give her plenty of local color to put into her stories, but just in time he remembered that the barman there, Jake, knew him to be a federal deputy, and Longarm had said nothing to Jake about keeping that a secret. At the time he had not thought that might be desirable.

So he steered Millicent past the Palace and entered a somewhat less fancy place a few doors beyond. A sign over the sidewalk proclaimed the establishment to be the Silver Cask.

Millicent's grip tightened on Longarm's arm as they

54

walked through the doors, and she looked positively en-
thralled by the unfamiliar sights and odors of the saloon.

Fulfilling its name, there was a small cask of chased
silver mounted on an ornately carved shelf behind the bar,
and the place was at least nice enough to boast a brass rail
and a set of mirrors flanking the silver cask behind the bar.

There were also, Longarm noted with some embarrassment, art works on the wall depicting plump, naked women
in various artistic poses, all of which contrived to display
their uncovered bosoms and dimpled navels.

"Maybe I should've warned you," Longarm apologized.
"I never thought . . ."

"Don't be silly," Millicent said with a laugh. "I've seen
a naked woman before, Custis. I have a mirror, you know."

He grinned at her. "What you see in your mirror is better'n anything you'll see on a saloon wall."

It was Millicent's turn to blush with a quick show of
embarrassment.

Although it was scarcely past eight o'clock in the morning, the bar was lined with drinkers, probably foremen and
shift supervisors, judging both from their dress and their
choice of saloons, Longarm thought. The gaming tables
were also noisily busy. Mining camps, however big or solidly established, never seemed to sleep.

Millicent clung to his arm, her head swiveling rapidly
from side to side as she tried to take in everything at once.

The odors of fresh beer and stale tobacco, spilled liquor
and ancient sweat, were comfortingly familiar to Longarm,
but to the girl they would have been new and exotically
exciting. Longarm found that he was rather enjoying watching Millicent's joyous responses to the wonder of it all. Her
face was alive with the pleasure she took in being able to
investigate this strange, forbidden territory.

Over by the bar there was something being displayed
other than joy at her presence.

As soon as they entered there was a slackening in the
flow of talk, a change of pitch and tempo to the buzz of

many conversations, and heads turned toward them from every direction.

Most of the customers were too polite to stare, but the bartender, a fat man with a walrus moustache and very little hair above eyebrow level glared at them openly. He quite obviously did not like this intrusion of a female into the sacrosanct territory of the male.

"You don't want to go up by that bar, Milly," Longarm said.

"But—"

"You can see everything you need from farther away." Quickly Longarm guided her away from the conspicuous doorway and toward the side of the room where there was, fortunately, a table available.

He tried to seat Millicent so that her back would be to the busy room, but she would have none of that. She insisted on being able to see everything.

Longarm, unwilling to expose his back to a room full of strangers, compromised by turning the square table at an angle to the wall so they could sit more or less side by side with the solid wall panels behind them.

The precaution did not go unremarked by the girl, and Longarm was reminded that she was cute but not necessarily stupid.

"You are a very cautious man, Custis."

He grunted.

"I keep thinking of the way you woke up last night," she went on, "with that gun in your hand, when I hadn't hardly made a peep of sound."

He grunted again.

"You know, Custis, you never have told me just what it is you do."

"What would you like, Milly?" It was an awfully crude way to change the subject and unlikely to put her off for long, but he could not think of anything else at the moment short of lying to her. And he did not want to do that.

She gave him an indulgent smile but apparently decided

56

to respect his privacy, at least for the moment. "What are you having?" she asked.

"Beer, I reckon."

"A beer for me, too, then."

"You're sure?" She hardly seemed the type to swill beer at any time of day, much less so early in the morning.

Millicent smiled. "You've already taught me so much, Custis. I might as well have another new experience." She blushed slightly at the memory of all that implied.

Longarm grinned at her. "You're the reporter. Whatever you say." He left her alone at the table and headed for the bar. He was quite sure the barman's unhappy look in their direction meant they were not going to get any table service in the Silver Cask.

"Two beers," he said, hooking an elbow onto the seldom-polished surface of the bar.

The barman ignored him and turned to pour a shot of red whiskey for another man nearby.

"Say, friend—"

The barkeep shot him an angry look, then turned away again.

Longarm's polite expression hardened, and his eyes became steely. He took a step forward along the bar front and shouldered the whiskey drinker out of his way.

His arm flashed forward and his fist formed an iron grip on the open throat of the bartender's collarless shirt. "I was speaking to you, friend." His voice was icily cold.

The barman glanced his way this time, and the man's hand began to dip beneath the top of his bar. But he got a good look at Longarm's face and his motion stopped abruptly.

The man's face worked with some difficulty, finally arriving at a weak semblance of a smile. "Guess I didn't hear you."

Longarm released his hold on the man's shirtfront and gave him a thin-lipped smile that had no warmth in it whatsoever. "I'm sure it was just an oversight."

"Yes, sir." The bartender trembled a little when he pulled

back on the tall wooden handle of his tap to draw a pair of beers into heavy glass mugs.

Longarm's inclination was to apologize. It was not like him to intimidate people—at least not those who had broken no laws—and he felt a little uncomfortable with the knowledge that he had done exactly that.

Still, it was Millicent the fat man was insulting, and Longarm was not going to stand for that. It was an unhappy dilemma the girl had forced on him here.

He accepted the beers, their heads a careful inch and no more, he noted, and paid his dime.

When he turned back toward their table, he discovered that Millicent was no longer alone.

Some snappily dressed son of a bitch was standing over the girl's chair and saying something to her.

Scowling and ready to fight, Longarm hurried across the room toward the girl and whoever that fool was.

Chapter 7

"Please, Carl, I am *not*—" Millicent saw Longarm approach and stopped what she was saying, giving the tall deputy a look of relief.

The little he had overheard on his way to the table, though, took away some of his impulse toward quick anger with the man. At least the fellow, whoever he was, seemed to know the girl. He was not just some yahoo making an assumption about Millicent's morals simply because she was here inside the Silver Cask.

Longarm set the two mugs on the table and stood beside Millicent's chair, interposing himself between her and the man who had been talking to her.

Longarm gave the fellow a good looking over. Whoever he was, he dressed well. He had on a suit of steel gray in some expensive-looking material and a Stetson of almost the exact same shade. His starched linen collar was crisp and unsmudged, and he wore a carefully knotted, wide tie beneath a dark red vest. He was wearing boots instead of shoes, Longarm saw, and a diamond stickpin winked brightly

59

from its nest in the cloth of his tie under a clean-shaven chin.

He was a handsome son of a bitch, Longarm admitted, and was tall enough to stand eye to eye with the deputy. But Longarm thought that stickpin looked like an awfully gaudy bauble for a grown man to decorate himself with.

Longarm had not noticed at first glance, but a pair of slight bulges under each arm meant that the man was either carrying twin pistols in shoulder harnesses or he was built damned funny in the chest. Longarm had a suspicion which way that would turn out to be.

"This is my escort, Mr. Long, Carl," Millicent said primly. "Custis, this is Carl Deeb."

Longarm nodded an acknowledgement of the introduction. Neither man expressed any pleasure at the meeting.

"As I was saying, Carl, I do not wish to have dinner with you. Thank you for the invitation, I'm sure, but I decline, as I shall decline any further invitations as well. Is that mine, Custis? Thank you." She flashed a smile, a rather strained smile, Longarm thought, toward him and reached to claim one of the mugs from the table. She took a sip of the bitter brew and fought hard to keep from making a face.

Longarm remembered the first time he had tasted beer. Back then he would likely not have believed he would ever come to enjoy the stuff; it was one of those tastes that definitely had to be acquired. Under other circumstances he would have found Millicent's efforts to control her expression amusing.

But a strong, if unreasoned, dislike for this Carl Deeb made him unwilling to show his amusement.

Longarm looked at Deeb through narrowed eyes and saw Deeb looking back at him with exactly the same kind of expression.

It could be like that sometimes, Longarm thought. Like two feists meeting in the street for the first time. The difference was that a pair of dogs were free to sniff and snarl and then have at each other. Civilized human beings were expected to limit themselves to a raising of the hackles and nothing more.

Longarm looked at Deeb and intensely disliked him and knew equally well that the feeling was returned in full.

They were two tall, good-looking men who despised each other on sight, and Millicent Cater's presence had nothing more to do with it than being an excuse. It was as simple as that.

"Custis, huh?" Deeb asked. He did not bother to try to hide the slight upward curl of his lip into a sneer when he spoke the name.

"That's right. Custis Long."

"Funny name, Custis."

"Meaning?"

Deeb tilted his head back to peer at Longarm down a patrician nose. The sneer had not left his face. "Just commenting. That's all. Custis." His mouth worked from side to side as if he found the name distasteful. Probably he did.

Longarm bridled. But he had years of practice and let none of that show. His expression remained mild and passive. Only the coldly impassive depths of his eyes gave any indication of what he was feeling.

Deeb seemed fully capable of reading that controlled anger, though. His head tipped back even further, and he gave a condescendingly superior bark of laughter at Longarm's unwillingness to cause a disturbance in Millicent's presence.

"I want to talk to you. *Custis.*"

Longarm wanted to chop this supercilious bastard down to size. Dwarf size. But both Millicent and his sense of duty—he was here to do a job and not to get into private fights, however much he might enjoy them—kept him outwardly calm. "Go right ahead," he said mildly.

Deeb looked at him and grinned. The handsome bastard might well have misinterpreted Longarm's reluctance to respond to his ill-mannered tone.

"In private," Deeb said arrogantly. He began to turn

61

away, then stopped. "No, on second thought, perhaps this should not be in private. I want Miss Cater to understand the way things are going to be, too. *Custis.*" He managed to make the name sound like a dirty word.

"Then I hope your language will be appropriate for the ears of a lady," Longarm said.

"Oh, of course." Deeb smiled. He seemed to be enjoying himself. He also seemed to feel very much in control of the situation. Apparently he had decided that Custis Long was no threat to him and he could do as he wished. "Sit down." He motioned Longarm toward a chair at his own table.

Meekly, Longarm sat. He leaned back in the chair and folded his hands across his stomach. It was not exactly deliberately provocative, but Longarm was not exactly forgetful either that his hand lay close beside the butt of his Colt in that position.

Deeb took a seat across the table from Longarm and the girl. He leaned back with his fingers lightly holding the lapels of his finely tailored suit. That, Longarm realized, kept *his* hands close to his pistols.

It was also a pity, Longarm thought, that neither of them could do what they really wanted to do.

"The way it is, *Custis,* I'm the man you have to please around here."

"Really?"

"Really. And you'd best remember it. You being seen in public with Miss Cater doesn't please me, Custis. Not in a place like this. Not in any place."

"I take it there's an understanding between you and the lady, then?" Longarm asked.

A faint gasp beside him made Millicent's version of the answer quite clear.

"So to speak," Deeb said. "Not that it's any of your business, Custis." He smiled. Longarm thought his smile a rather ugly expression. "Whatever happens between Miss Cater and me, Custis, you aren't to worry yourself about

62

it. That's what I want to get across to you. Before you get yourself in trouble here, boy. You got to think about these things, you know."

"Maybe my thinking's a bit thick this morning," Longarm said, "but I don't think I understand you."

Deeb's self-satisfied smile turned to a look of raw hatred, and he leaned forward intently. "Hands off, buster, or I'll make more trouble for you than you could ever imagine."

"Somehow, Carl, I kinda doubt that," Longarm said softly.

"Believe it, mister," Deeb snarled. He reached inside his coat. It was unlikely that the man knew how close he came to dying at that moment, because his attention was momentarily distracted by the search for his own wallet.

He pulled out a badge, not a gun, and flipped it onto the table between them. "You see that, Custis? That right there says when I snap, you jump. And you jump just as high an' just as far as I want, or you'll regret you ever came here, boy."

"My oh my," Longarm said. "A deputy. My oh my." Quite deliberately he chuckled his lack of respect for the Storey County deputy's badge that lay on the table.

Deeb was furious. "Listen to me, boy. You're new here. If you weren't you'd already know the way things are. You don't look like a salesman. Prob'ly some tinhorn engineer. Not that it makes any difference. Not to me, it doesn't. Not around here. I don't care who you are, *Custis,* or how bad you *used* to think you were. Around here, you don't have a job, any job, unless I say you can. Around here, boy, you get a step out of line and I pass the word to the mines. They hire you and they'll be violating half the laws on the books. I'll see to it. And I'll make it stick. *Now* do you understand me? *Custis?*"

Longarm was almost enjoying this now.

Oh, it was quite a performance Deputy Deeb was giving. Hell, he probably meant it. He probably even *could* do everything he said. And would do it.

63

Longarm felt a coppery, acid taste come into his mouth. Now he had a reason, a damned good reason, for feeling the way he did toward Carl Deeb.

A peace officer had enough to put up with without some sorry son of a bitch like this giving the breed a well-earned bad name.

Bastard.

Longarm looked across the table toward Deeb again, and something Jake Jacobs had said the night before registered. This right here was the lying, chiseling bullyboy of a deputy who had collected another man's reward money and spent it on a diamond stickpin and a new suit of clothes. Jacobs had not mentioned any names, but now that Longarm had met the good Deputy Deeb no names were needed.

Longarm looked at Deeb and laughed in his face.

"You just made a real bad mistake. Custis."

Longarm laughed again. "Somehow, Carl, I don't really think so. Go easy now. I'm not reaching for a gun." Longarm pulled his own wallet out and flipped it open. "Make all the trouble you want, Carl. Give it your very best shot. But the fact is, I carry a bigger stick than you do. Mess with Miss Cater... *boy*... or with me, and I'll reach down your throat and pile your liver and lights in an alley for the dogs to chew on. You got my word on the subject. *Boy*."

Deeb blanched an unhealthy pale beneath his tan when he saw Longarm's federal identification. His mouth worked like a banked fish sucking air. Longarm guessed the son of a bitch wanted to say something full of threat and bluster but all of a sudden didn't know what that might be.

The man regained some measure of control over himself. He stood and snatched his shiny badge from the table. He glared first at Longarm, then at Millicent. Without another word he turned and stalked out of the Silver Cask at a pace that was just short of a run.

The early morning drinkers, Longarm noticed, seemed to be thoroughly enjoying the sight of the bully deputy in flight.

Longarm reached out to retrieve his own badge, and the thought came to him.

Son of a bitch! If he had wanted to remain inconspicuous, he had sure taken care of that. And if he wanted to keep the pretty little would-be reporter from knowing who he was, he had sure as hell torn that as well. And if he wanted to keep the local law from knowing he was around for another day or two, well, it looked like his luck was on a real roll here. *Everything* had gone bust in that respect.

Damn. He tucked his wallet away, gave Millicent a nervous smile, and took a swallow of the lukewarm beer that he had not yet touched.

Some days, he thought, it just didn't pay a fellow to get out of bed.

Chapter 8

"Why didn't you tell me . . . ?"

"Shhhh. Not now. Finish your— No, never mind that.
Let's go back to the hotel room so we can talk without
everybody staring at us."

Millicent giggled, and Longarm got the distinct impression that her idea of going back to the hotel room was not
entirely the same as his. He did want to talk to her in private,
though. He left his beer almost untouched on the table, and
they went back up to the Buckhorn.

"Now," he said as soon as the door was locked behind
them.

He turned to the girl, fully intending to have a conversation with her, but Millicent obviously wanted another form
of communication first.

She put her arms around his neck before he could say
anything more and covered his mouth with hers even though
she had to practically pull him down into a stooping position
to reach him. Her hips were moving in a quite unladylike
manner against his groin, and Longarm decided that maybe
their talk could wait a little while.

She was breathing heavily before he could even get his coat and vest off, and when he laid his gunbelt aside and reached for his trouser buttons Millicent was there ahead of him.

"Let me."

"Mmmm?"

"What you showed me last night." She looked up at him and grinned.

Deftly—the result, he thought, of much practice with the tiny buttons that women's fashions seemed to favor— she freed him from the cloth.

Longarm was more than ready for her. He sprang free of the restraint, and his cock throbbed rigidly at attention.

Millicent dropped to her knees and spent several long, delicious moments caressing him. "Yum," she said.

"Are you sure you want to?"

"Absolutely." She leaned forward and ran the tip of her tongue lightly around the head of his tool, then down the length of it to swirl against his scrotum. She rocked back onto her heels and smiled. "Is that all right?"

"Rather."

"Good." She went back to her task, this time drawing him slowly into her mouth. He could feel the flicker of her tongue there, too, darting around and around while she held him inside.

"Damned good," Longarm agreed. Under the circumstances the formal proscription of profanity in a lady's company did not seem to apply.

He stroked her hair. It felt as soft and sleek and glossy as it looked.

Millicent withdrew from him for a moment and said, "Don't do that, please."

"I'm a long way from coming yet."

"Not that, silly. I won't mind swallowing it if you want to finish this way. But please don't mess up my hairdo. I'd have to repin it and everything." With a slurping, gurgling sound she went back to the business of pleasing him.

Son of a gun, Longarm thought. She didn't want her hair mussed. He was reasonably well convinced that, no matter what, he would *never* learn to understand women. Even *one* of the odd creatures, much less the whole kit and caboodle of them.

Longarm stood with his head back and his legs braced wide and let the girl have her way with him. He was not in any particular hurry to reach a climax, but the girl seemed to accept her task as a challenge, and he quickly met the demand of her hot mouth and greedy tongue.

He held himself still until the last possible second and then quivered only slightly at the delightful outpouring that sent its sensations racing from his scalp to his toenails.

He thought for a moment that Millicent was going to choke. The orgasm went on and on until he thought he must have spilled at least a pint of his seed into her. But she stayed with him the entire time, and when she finally did release him it was with a smile and a happy licking of her lips. Longarm shuddered with an after-explosion that was somewhat like a California earthquake.

"Damn, you're good," he said.

"Thank you." She came lightly to her feet and began to peel herself out of the involved tangle of clothing that polite custom dictated she wear in public. "My turn now, Custis?"

"You bet." He stretched out on the bed and waited for her.

"Thank you for solving my problem with Carl."

They were lying on top of the bedcovers, Millicent as shamelessly naked in the full daylight as Longarm was. At the moment she was running her fingertips across his chest while she lay propped on one elbow with her abundant breasts plastered against his side. The contact felt quite good in spite of his currently limp condition of overuse.

"I take it you didn't have any sort of understanding with him?"

"Of course not, though I haven't been able to convince *him* of that. The man's a snake, Custis."

So much for any theories about women not being able to see past a handsome rascal's face. He agreed with her.

"What happened," Millicent said, "is that he saw me at the *Enterprise* office one day and . . . well, I guess he took something of a shine to me. He said he did, anyway. I didn't want to have anything to do with him, and I told him so. That might have been a mistake. Certainly he has pestered me at every opportunity since then."

She made a sour face. "Why, that man even had the nerve to suggest that he could get me a position with the newspaper if I agreed to be 'nice' to him." She shuddered. "I can just imagine what *that* would mean."

The girl was no prude, Longarm thought. Not lying there sweat-sheened from their recent lovemaking and very fetchingly naked, she wasn't. What it meant, he decided, was that the girl simply had excellent taste in male companionship. He smiled to himself.

"I imagine he really could get me a job, and of course I do want a job. But not that way." She snuggled closer to Longarm. "The fact is that I am really quite satisfied for the moment, just the way things are."

After a brief pause Millicent sat bolt upright on the bed beside him. She let out a sharp little yelp and hit him lightly on the chest.

"Hey, what is that about?"

"You," she accused. "How could I have forgotten? You, Custis Long. Why, I swear you are as much a snake in the grass as that Carl is. Maybe worse."

"Me?" Longarm asked in all innocence.

"You," she affirmed. "You *knew* I would want to write a story about you when I learned what you do. That is exactly why you wouldn't tell me."

"Can't deny it," Longarm agreed. "It's the truth." He reached for his hastily discarded coat and fished in the

69

pockets for a cheroot. There was nothing like a good smoke after a good screwing.

Millicent must not have been too angry, he observed. She took the box of lucifers from beside the bedside lamp and lit the cigar for him.

Longarm plumped up the pillow behind his neck and settled back with a sigh of contentment. "Now," he said, "I believe we were in the middle of a fight or something. What was it about again?" He grinned at her.

She tried to give him a look of outraged anger, but she just could not bring it off. She began to laugh instead.

"Really, darling, you should have told me."

"Really, pretty girl, I couldn't," he replied.

"Why?"

"You already said it yourself. I'm here to do a job, Milly. I can't have you tagging around with me every step of the way. Completely aside from the fact that the men I'm after are dangerous, which I don't think for a minute would deter you—"

"It wouldn't," she interrupted.

"Exactly. But, quite apart from that, being with you makes me stand out from the crowd. I can't afford that. And it makes it awkward for me to go into the places I'll have to go to look for these people. If I travel around with you all the time, or if you're hanging around outside the doors waiting to pounce on me every time I come outside, it would cause an awful lot of stir. By this time tomorrow everybody in Virginia City would know who I am and what I'm here for. I can't have that, Milly. I can't afford to spook these men and let them get away."

"They are real desperadoes, Custis?"

He could not help but laugh at the eager way her green eyes widened and at her using that dime-novel term for some plain old criminals. "Yes," he said, "they are real desperadoes."

She swung her legs around so she could sit cross-legged facing him. She looked quite pretty sitting there with her face alive with excitement and her other charms on full display. Longarm noticed, though, that her hair had gotten disheveled in spite of her concern for it. "Tell me about them," she urged.

He shrugged. "There won't be that much to tell unless I can find them."

"What are they wanted for?"

"The leader's wanted for murder, the others for this and that crime, one place or another."

"Murder!" Millicent's eyes gleamed. "Truly?"

"That's what's written on the warrant."

"Oh, Custis, I simply *must* be able to write this story. It could mean *everything* to me. Think about it. An *exclusive* story with the western manhunter who is bringing a real-life murderer to justice. Why, there isn't a newspaper in the East that wouldn't just *have* to buy that story. It could be the start of my whole *career*."

"Which, if you will remember, was my objection to letting you know what I do for a living, Milly. I just can't have you interfering with this."

"But—"

"No, Milly. No buts. If you can't stay out of my way voluntarily, I'll have to think of some way to make you stay away. I don't want to do that. And I certainly want you to do well with this reporting stuff. But I just can't allow a murderer to escape on your account."

Millicent looked glum. She pouted and muttered a few words that Longarm would not have thought she would know. Then she brightened. "I have an idea," she said.

"Such as?"

"I'll agree to stay completely out of your way. Out of sight even. But you have to agree to two things, Custis."

"Mmm?"

"One is that as soon as your job is done, you will sit down with me and give me all the particulars about it. All of them, mind, every little bit. The other is— Well, I can't go back to my room or anything unless I find a job some-

71

where, and if I am to concentrate on this story I can't very well be out looking for a job, can I? What I mean is..."

"I know what you mean." Longarm wondered if this would fall into the line-of-duty classification the next time some beureaucratic auditor got around to looking at the Denver district's books. He definitely hoped that it would.

"One other thing you have to promise, Milly," he told her.

"What?" She sounded wary.

"You can stay here as long as I keep the room. And if you really do stay out of my way you can have the story when I'm done. But there is one other thing that I absolutely insist on, or it's no deal. When you write your story for those eastern papers, Milly, I want you to use some made-up name instead of mine."

"Custis! Really? I could make you *famous*. Why, I could make you more famous than Wyatt Earp."

"I think so, too, and that, my girl, is exactly what I'm afraid of. I've met Mr. Earp, and I've heard all the opinions about him too, and I just don't think I want to be seen in that same light. I'm happy the way things are, thank you."

"Are you sure, Custis?"

"That's the deal, Milly. Take it or don't."

She sighed. "I'll take it."

"It's a promise?"

"I promise. I'll stay out of your way. And I won't use your name. And you will tell me absolutely everything there is to tell when you're done."

"Agreed." They shook hands on it.

Millicent laughed and let out a short yip of happiness.

"What was that about?"

"What was it *about?* Silly man. Why, you have just guaranteed, I mean positively *guaranteed,* that I will be able to sell a story, finally. And, I might add, in the meantime I get to make passionate," she fondled him, "and frequent love to a *real* U. S. marshal."

"Just a deputy," he corrected.

"Don't quibble, dear." She bent over him, her falling hair tickling the insides of his thighs. "Not at a time like this."

What the hell, Longarm thought. It was tough duty, but someone had to do it.

Chapter 9

"I'm thinking about sending a complaint to Washington. A formal complaint. About you."

Longarm crossed his arms and waited. There seemed little point in trying to say or explain anything. Sheriff D. K. Randolph was just plain mad. Much too mad to listen to reason, particularly when any real reasons Longarm might choose to give would not reflect well on the sheriff's personnel.

The man's tirade had been going on for some little time now, and Longarm was frankly tired of it. But he did not know a better way to handle it than to simply ride it out.

In the meantime Deputy Carl Deeb was having himself a hell of a good time listening to the big-shot federal man get his butt chewed.

Deeb was standing to one side of the sheriff's desk, smirking and grinning behind his boss's back while Randolph blew off anger at Longarm's tardiness in checking in with the local authorities.

Bastard, Longarm thought. He found it much more interesting to think about finding an excuse to have a private

74

"discussion" with Deeb than to listen to Randolph yammering.

There was another deputy present too. Longarm wondered if Randolph was so unsure of himself that he felt a need to have some of his own people on hand for protection, either physical or emotional, while he cussed out the interloper.

Except for the quality of his bluster, D. K. Randolph did not impress Longarm a whole hell of a lot.

The man must have been in his late sixties or early seventies, which in itself was no indictment of his abilities, but it was fairly obvious that he was going to seed.

Whatever he might have been in the past—and Longarm had no way to judge that now—at present his face showed the florid, heavily veined complexion of a man who was drinking altogether too much, and the mottled red coloring of his skin implied that he might have other physical problems as well. His clothes were liberally dotted with stains and dribbles of cigar ash and who knew what other indignities.

Looking at Randolph, Longarm thought, could be a case in itself against county sheriffs reaching office through the political process.

D. K. Randolph struck him as being a political hack of the worst sort. And in an office like this, such a man could be a positive danger to his commity. It was a damned shame.

The deputy who flanked the sheriff on the side opposite Deeb was an unknown quantity. There had been no introductions when Longarm was summoned to this audience, and as far as Longarm could remember now the deputy had remained completely silent throughout the harangue.

The deputy was short, five-foot-five or thereabouts, but he did not carry himself with the cocky, gun-quick swagger so many short men seemed to adopt as a form of compensation for their diminutive size. Longarm approved of that about him. And he knew when to keep his mouth shut, obviously.

Not as much could be said for Deputy Deeb. Throughout

the sheriff's whining complaints and silly accusations, Deeb had been quick to jump in at any opportunity and add fuel to the fire.

By now, Longarm thought, enough accusations, complaints, and downright lies had been spouted in this office that it would take a bright and fair-minded man days to sort them all out. Randolph, it was clear, would have no interest in even trying.

So Longarm sat in politely respectful silence and waited for the nattering to end. Then he could go on about his business.

"No respect, no *courtesy*, by God, an' this right here is the backbone o' the whole, entire damn system, mister federal man. You think about that, boy. This right here's the backbone o' the system. Why, it's me and my boys here that have t' do all the work, day in an' day out, an' you glory boys from Washington—"

"Denver," Longarm corrected softly.

"Wherever. You glory boys . . . what the hell was I saying?" Randolph turned to Deeb.

"No respect for real lawmen," the deputy was happy to suggest.

"Right. No respect at all." The sheriff ran down for a moment and paused to wipe his forehead with a handkerchief that was long overdue for laundering.

"I might point out," Longarm said, "that this is my first day in your town. And the fact remains, no harm has been done."

He smiled and let Randolph respond at some incoherent length. Longarm only hoped that it was true that no harm had been done.

He had had his doubts before, based on the informant's decision not to tip the plan to the Stoney County law. After meeting Randolph and Deeb, he was even more concerned about the security of this investigation.

Randolph might be one of those bad apples in the law

enforcement barrel or he might as easily be just an aging incompetent. Longarm had no way to judge that.

About Deeb he had even more reservations. A man who would steal a reward might well be willing to steal on a grander scale.

As far as Longarm could tell it wasn't how many dollars were stolen that made the crime, it was the fact of theft itself. Stealing a dime was just as wrong as stealing a fortune. The difference was only one of degree.

Longarm's fear now was that by letting the Storey County people in on this, as he had been forced to do, he had at the same time tipped the Professor and his crowd that the law was onto them.

That, he knew, could be dangerous.

He sat quietly and listened to the rest of the sheriff's complaints, few of which made any apparent sense, and eventually the man ran out of things to whine about.

"I'll be sure to keep your department fully informed of the progress of my investigation," Longarm said when Randolph was finally done. Any reservations he might have had about that he kept to himself.

"See that you do, boy, or I'll damn sure send that complaint on to Washington." The poor man seemed to think that was quite a threat. It was not. Billy Vail did not allow his people to be intimidated by anyone, including anyone a hell of lot higher up on the political ladder than this broken down has-been seemed to be.

"I appreciate your situation here, Sheriff Randolph, and I will be glad to cooperate with your men. I know you have a difficult job to do, and I'm sure you are doing it very well." It never hurt to pour oil on the waters. Longarm almost choked on the words, but none of his true feelings showed in his voice or expression.

Randolph grunted. He probably would have responded favorably to some outright flattering, but Longarm just wasn't in the mood for it.

77

"If you will excuse me now?" Longarm stood and extended his hand to the elected sheriff. He nodded to the short deputy and flashed Deeb a cocky grin before he turned and left the courthouse.

Longarm stopped at the courthouse door to get a breath of fresh air and to light a cheroot. It had been stuffy in the office and although the air in there stank of stale tobacco smoke Longarm had chosen not to antagonize the old fossil any further by smoking in his office. He took a deep pull on the cigar and drew the smoke into his lungs. It tasted clean and good after the foul surroundings of Randolph's office.

"Marshal Long?"

He turned. "Yes?"

The small deputy had come out of the courthouse behind him. The man stepped forward now and offered his hand.

"Hank Bigelow," he introduced himself. He settled a hardcrowned derby onto his head and for a moment looked uncertain of how he wanted to go on now that he had come forward. "Would you have a moment?" he asked hesitantly.

"I reckon."

"Would you like a drink, then?" Bigelow grinned. "I think I could use one myself."

Longarm shrugged. "Sure."

They walked together down to the level of the business district. Bigelow pulled a pipe from his coat pocket and filled and lighted it while they walked. He led the way into a small but quite elegantly appointed saloon on the lower street level.

Longarm headed in the direction of the gleaming bar, but the deputy touched him on the arm and guided him instead toward a table isolated in a corner. "This might be quieter."

"All right."

Bigelow definitely had something on his mind, Longarm thought. The question was what.

As a precaution Longarm took the chair back in the corner

and surveyed the room for any possible sign of trouble. He could see nothing out of the ordinary, but he did not relax his caution.

Bigelow waited until Longarm was done with his examination of their surroundings. Then he sighed. "I guess I can't blame you for being suspicious, Marshal," he said.

"Suspicious? Naw. Nothing to fret about around here, is there?"

Bigelow swallowed. "Look, Marshal, I don't know how to say this right. I mean . . . well, I try to do my job the best I can. And there's others in the department that do the same. We *care*. Do you know what I mean?"

Longarm looked at the man more closely. Bigelow's expression was open and honest and . . . it took Longarm a moment to peg it . . . anguished.

Anybody can be taken in by an honest-looking crook, deputy U. S. marshals included, but Longarm did not think that was the case here. Hank Bigelow really did care about the job he was trying to do. Longarm felt reasonably sure of that.

And, he realized, it was a hard place the man was in here. A stranger, a federal officer, had just seen his department's boss and chief deputy at their worst. The warts were all on public display. Yet a conscientious lawman would not want to be disloyal to his own department. Longarm understood that.

"I think I know what you mean, Hank." He used the deputy's first name deliberately, as a signal of sorts. He did not want to make it worse for Bigelow by speaking openly about just how lousy the department's leadership was.

"What I was thinking . . ." Bigelow began. He stopped. "Look, Marshal, could this talk be just . . . well . . . between the two of us? Go no further than that?"

Longarm nodded. "You can have my word on it."

"Okay."

Longarm stopped him from saying anything more at the moment. An aproned waiter was approaching the table.

Bigelow ordered a beer. Longarm was ready for something a damn sight stronger, so he ordered Maryland rye.

"Like I said, this is between the two of us," Longarm affirmed when the waiter was gone.

"Good." Bigelow stared at his hands for a moment. "There are some real good boys in this department, Marshal," he said. "You ought to know that."

Longarm smiled at him. "I haven't met but a few. I can believe I've met at least one good one."

Hank Bigelow gave him a smile in return that was both relief and thanks. "Deke—Sheriff Randolph, that is—he didn't ask you for much information about this case you're on. An' I can understand how you might want to keep it to yourself. Things bein' the way they are and all. But I want you to know, if there's anything me or the other boys can do to help . . . well, we'll turn our butts inside out to try and find this fella you're after. I want you to know that, Marshal."

"Why don't you call me Longarm? That's a lot less formal than a title."

Bigelow smiled at him again.

Their drinks came, and Bigelow sipped at his beer. Longarm downed the shot of Maryland rye and ordered another. It tasted awfully good.

"I think," Longarm said, "you're going to need some information if you intend to help with the investigation. Do you know a man called the Professor? The name is really T. Anthony Scott. Anything ring a bell there? Or how about a one-legged man called Duck?"

Bigelow shook his head.

"Let me start at the front then and tell you the whole thing." He sketched in the entire story, holding nothing back that could relate to the Professor and his planned robbery.

If any damage had already been done with Randolph, Longarm reasoned, the rest of the facts could do no additional harm. And with this Hank Bigelow he thought there was at least a chance that the local people might actually help. Longarm was far from being too proud to accept assistance from a local officer.

"I can tell you this, Longarm," Bigelow said when Longarm was done talking. "I don't personally know of anyone who might be the Professor, although with him being so expert at disguise I wouldn't want to say for sure, of course. I'll damn sure put the word out on him, though.

"As for the others you know about, Al Higgins could be here using another name and we'd not have a line on him. And this Duck Bragg fellow . . . well, there's a lot of men missing a leg or an arm in any mining town. I expect you know that. I don't happen to know of any using that name, but I'll sure check around. If any of us finds anything, I'll let you know right off. You can count on that."

Longarm smiled. "I believe I can, Hank."

They finished their drinks, and Longarm paid, over Bigelow's protests.

"My treat, Hank." He grinned. "Aside from the fact that it's on the expense voucher, it's always a pleasure to meet a good officer, wherever I find one."

That seemed to please the small deputy.

Chapter 10

Longarm stood at the bar, elbowed in among many other drinkers in the noisy saloon, and tried to fight off a case of the grumps.

It seemed like it had taken him half of forever to get to a point where he could finally begin doing some actual work on this investigation. And now that he was, he felt more useless than ever.

He had spent the entire evening wandering from one saloon and gambling house to another. He had left countless half-full beers on who knew how many bars.

And he had accomplished not a damn thing.

T. Anthony Scott. *Professor* T. Anthony Scott. Longarm could well have stood right beside the bastard and had a beer with him and not known it.

Longarm was not even certain he would still recognize the Professor if the man was wearing no disguise at all. And if he had chosen to disguise himself, the task would be next to impossible.

Longarm wondered if his only real hope of finding the man would be to hold himself out as bait, let the Professor recognize him and try to kill him. It was not a cheering prospect.

Besides, a man as bright as he remembered Scott to be might well rely on the safety of his disguise and simply walk away, unsuspected, into the night instead of trying to make a break for it with a gun in his hand.

Damn, Longarm thought.

It was almost as bad trying to spot Duck Bragg.

A fellow would think that anything as obvious as a one-legged man would be a snap to find. Not so.

So far this evening Longarm had spotted three men missing arms and two missing legs. Of the two who were one-legged—and, damn it, why had that flyer not specified *which* leg was missing?—one was a down-and-out rummy on the elderly side who could not possibly have had the steady hands necessary for a powder man, and the other was a nattily dressed professional gambler who probably made more money in one good night at the tables than a train robber could hope for in his share from half a dozen holdups.

Train robbery, Longarm knew, was highly overrated as a source of income.

Come to think of it, though, he thought now, if the Professor was interested enough in this shipment to make it his last bid for freedom, it would have to be an extraordinary haul.

Perhaps, Longarm thought, the approach he should take here was not the gang members but their target. He made a mental note to himself to call on the mine operators tomorrow, when their offices should be open. The mines would be operating day and night, of course, but the offices could be expected to keep normal hours.

He felt a little better after he decided that. Not much, but a little better.

"Another?" the bartender asked.

Longarm shook his head.

"If you're done, mister, make way for someone else."

"Sure." Longarm turned and idled out of the saloon. He was not accomplishing anything there anyway.

The air outside was cool and refreshing. There was a faint tinge of chemical stink to it, but nothing serious. Longarm assumed it had something to do with the chemicals used to amalgamate the crushed ore or some other equally obscure process having to do with mining. Longarm had spent some time swinging a singlejack underground, but that hardly gave him an in-depth knowledge of the minerals extraction processes, and at this point in time he really did not want to know any more about it than was necessary. The law was a much more interesting line of work, in his opinion, and most of the time it could even be considered much less dangerous. Hard-rock miners, he had long since decided, were a breed apart.

He lighted another cheroot, but the round of saloons and drinks had left him smoking one after another and the taste was foul in his mouth. He puffed on it only a few times before rubbing the coal free against the side of a building and putting the cheroot back into his pocket. He would smoke the thing later when he could enjoy it. He sighed and started down the street.

All around him Virginia City was busy. Men in mud-spattered overalls hurried along the sidewalks next to men in business suits and others dressed in little better than rags. Any and every class and social station was represented here. All seemed equally intent on their pleasures. None seemed more than passingly aware of how the other fellow was dressed. Democracy in action, Longarm thought with a thin smile; grab what you can and raise hell. The rich ores being dragged from the earth here were there for the taking, so grab them and enjoy them before it all ran out. In spite of Virginia City's long and solid past as a producer of the valuable metals, that still appeared to be the prevailing attitude in the wide-open town. If it had not been for the Professor—whose peculiarly bent attitudes might be considered just an extension of the general mood of the city,

84

Longarm might have found it all refreshing for its basically honest greed. But then there was that one little fly in the ointment that he had to consider.

He poked along the street, and his thoughts had begun to return to Millicent Cater. By this late hour she should have finished whatever it was she had been up to during the afternoon. She should be waiting for him at the Buckhorn. If his expectations were met there, she would be warm and willing and eager. The remainder of the night should be pleasant, even if the evening had been dreary.

He passed a dance hall where grimy miners laughed and shouted while they drank and paid scantily dressed girls five cents per tune to dance with them. Longarm glanced through the door toward the men without envy. It was only a deep-rooted, lonesome emptiness that would prompt a man to pay a girl just so he could hold her in his arms for the length of the dance. Yet for these miners the dance hall seemed to serve a purpose and assuage a need that the whorehouses could not. Certainly the two could operate successfully side by side, and each would be well attended.

Further up the street Longarm saw a familiar figure come out of a saloon and turn toward him. From the way the man was walking, not entirely steady on his pins, Longarm got the impression that Deputy Carl Deeb had been doing some fairly serious drinking. On the house, no doubt, Longarm reflected sourly. There was just something about the man that he did not like.

It was clear, though, that the feeling was mutual, and Longarm had no inclination at all to get into a fuss with the likes of Deputy Deeb. To avoid a confrontation that could prove nothing constructive, Longarm stepped aside into the darkened doorway of a barber-surgeon's shop. It seemed the prudent thing to do if not really the most satisfying course of action.

Deeb reached the steps leading from the sidewalk down to the mouth of an alley. He lurched slightly, stopped, and looked cautiously around. Then, instead of crossing the dark alley's mouth, he turned and headed across the street toward the opposite sidewalk, coming within thirty feet or so of Longarm's shadowed shape, but not seeing him standing there.

Longarm frowned his distaste for the man and reached into his pocket for a cheroot before resuming his walk toward the Buckhorn and Millicent Cater's waiting charms. Across the street a second man stepped out of the shadows to join Deeb.

The newcomer was on crutches. And he had an empty trouser leg pinned up above where his missing knee should have been.

Longarm's hand fell to belt level, his desire for a smoke forgotten now.

Carl Deeb and the one-legged man stood close together for some time. Their heads bobbed, and from time to time they gestured with their hands. Longarm could see their lips move, but at this distance there no way he could hope to overhear what they were saying, even if the saloons and gaming halls on the busy street had been silent.

Could the one-legged man possibly be...? Longarm shook his head impatiently. He did not want to jump to conclusions.

After a while the one-legged man tucked his right crutch under his arm and leaned on the left while he fished in his pockets. He brought something out—the lighting was too poor for Longarm to see what it was—and handed it to Deeb. Longarm practically groaned out loud with his desire to know what they had said and what had been passed from the one to the other. Deeb grinned and straightened his tie jauntily, then turned and walked back up the street. Longarm thought the bastard was walking much steadier now than he had been a few minutes earlier.

Longarm's mouth twisted in a bitter scowl. There were entirely too many unknowns here for him to reach any judgements or make any accusations. But *if*, damn it, Carl Deeb was doing what Custis Long suspected him of—well, there was little that disgusted Longarm worse than a lawman on the take.

Bastard, he thought.

It was the second man who interested Longarm now, the one-legged man. He could locate Deeb any time he wanted him. The other was a new and unknown quantity. When the one-legged man turned and crutched southward at a swift, well-practiced, swinging gait, Longarm trailed along behind him.

Pedestrian traffic on the partially lighted street was heavy, but Longarm had no trouble keeping his man in view. He stayed on his side of the street and ambled along the sidewalk whistling, without realizing it, the tune Brenda Savoit had sung back home in Denver.

The one-legged man neared the end of the business district, and Longarm thought for a moment that he was going to have difficulty following the fellow any further. The problem resolved itself when the suspect stopped to open a gate in an unpainted picket fence and let himself into the yard of an ornate house that barely showed any light through its heavily curtained windows. There was, Longarm noted with a smile, a lamp with a blood-red globe burning beside the front door of the place. Public enough, Longarm thought with satisfaction.

Longarm did not want to enter the whorehouse immediately on the heels—*make that heel,* he corrected—of the one-legged man, so he walked on for another hundred yards or so and found the bed of a parked wagon to lean against while he waited for a time and continued to keep an eye on the door of the place.

After a few minutes, enough time so that it would not seem he was coming right behind the one-legged man, he made his way back up the street to the low fence and creaky, unoiled gate in front of the nearly dark house. He knocked on the door.

"Yes, dearie? Come right in."

The invitation was extended by a heavily powdered woman

whose frizzy hair was a bright, artificial red. The woman looked too old to be one of the "girls," even in a mining camp, so Longarm assumed she was the madam or at least the manager of the place.

He was aware of the woman's scrutiny as she checked the cut of his clothing and his level of sobriety, obviously making sure he was suitable material for the house and probably as well determining his ability to pay.

"Howdy." Longarm plastered a broad, loose smile across his face and took his hat off before he stepped inside the house.

"Manners, too. My, I like that." The woman took his hat from him and remained immediately in front of him, blocking his entry beyond the vestibule. "Check your gun, too, dearie. We run a quiet place here. You won't need it."

Longarm dutifully unbuckled his gunbelt and allowed the woman to take his holstered Colt. He did not think it necessary, however, to mention the brass derringer that decorated one end of his watch chain in the place of a fob.

"Thank you, dearie. Come in to Sweet Belle's House of Joys."

`Chapter 11

The parlor of this parlor house, as the places were euphe-
mistically called by the classier folk, was a study in over-
done elegance. The furnishings were overstuffed, the
wallpaper flocked velvet, the room-sized rug damn near
ankle deep. Everything, but *every*thing, was done in red
and gold. Just about every damn thing that was made of a
fabric was deep red. Just about everything else was done
in gold leaf or had been painted gold. The effect, Longarm
thought, was rather overwhelming for a man whose tastes
were simple. But the customers seemed to like it.

The parlor held eight gentlemen—an obviously appropriate word for them, judging from the way they were
dressed—and half a dozen young, actually quite attractive
girls.

Unlike the cheaper joints where the whores might appear
on parade in sleazy kimonos or less, here the girls were in
gowns—low-cut and tight-waisted, to be sure, but gowns
nonetheless. Any of them could have moved from the House
of Joys to a grand ball and been appropriately dressed for
the occasion.

After seeing the one-legged man, that was a considerable

surprise. The one-legged man had not been dressed shabbily, exactly, but he was far from being in this class. The men who were lounging in the parlor when Longarm arrived had the look of supervisors or managers, even of mine owners. These men were obviously near the top of Virginia City's social structure. A one-legged train robber seemed hardly the type to be welcomed here. Yet it was perfectly clear that he had been. He had been admitted without question by the old harridan at the front door, and Longarm had not seen him come back out again. The obvious conclusion was that he was known here and was welcomed, or at least tolerated, for some reason that Longarm could not at the moment guess.

Longarm cleared his throat and stepped forward. He felt more than a little out of place here and reached for a cheroot to occupy his hands while he took stock of his surroundings.

Immediately there was a woman at his side with an engraved silver cigar clipper in one hand and a lighted match in the other. Longarm accepted her assistance and puffed his cheroot alight.

"Thank you, ma'am."

The woman nodded graciously. "You are quite welcome, sir. This is your first visit, I believe."

"It is," Longarm agreed.

He took a closer look at the woman. She was, he saw, somewhat older than the other girls, though not by much. He guessed her to be about thirty.

"I am Belle," she said with a smile.

"I thought . . . never mind." The red-haired old bag at the door, then, was just a dragon at the gates, he thought. A first line of defense against the unwashed and unwanted.

Belle smiled. She might have guessed what he had been thinking, but she did not comment on it.

"We want your visit here to be a joy," Belle said. "You should feel free to relax, visit with the ladies, have a drink if you wish. No one will hurry you."

"Thanks."

"Nor do we ever press you about mundane matters like money. A fee is collected on arrival. Fifty dollars, sir. That entitles you to the *intimate* visit with your choice of our young ladies. Tipping is not necessary, and I can assure you you will be entertained to your," she smiled, "satis-faction."

"It sounds very relaxed."

"Exactly. And we *do* want you to enjoy your visit with us. So if we can dispose of that one little matter I mentioned earlier . . . ?"

Fifty bucks up front. The working classes could get along on a dollar or so, but the upper crust was expected to pay considerably more for what was, when you got right down to it, basically the same privilege. Either way, the poor sap was just renting a place to put it.

Fifty dollars. That was going to tear hell out of the ex-pense money, and Billy Vail was sure to bark and snarl when he saw the accounting. Worse, Longarm was going to have to wire Vail for more money. Damn!

Still, the choice seemed to be to pay it or get out. And Longarm damn sure wanted to get a line on the gentleman who happened to have one leg and an association with Deputy Carl Deeb.

Longarm squelched the sigh that wanted to escape from his lips and dug deep into his dwindling roll of taxpayers' money.

"Thank you, sir," Belle said as she accepted the fee. "And I *do* hope you will enjoy yourself."

Longarm managed a smile and helped himself to a seat in an overstuffed chair with, inevitably, red upholstery and arms of carved, gilt wood. The chair was near a corner and from it he could keep an eye on the whole spacious room.

There were more customers in the parlor than girls, and all of the girls he could see were busy talking to what appeared to be their choice of men. They poured drinks mostly, Longarm noticed, from dusty wine and champagne bottles, and humidors of fat, pale-leafed cigars were frequently offered.

A doorway leading toward the back of the house seemed to be the avenue toward the promised joys, because it was in that direction that a girl would occasionally lead one of the gentlemen.

Once in a while, too, a couple would return to the parlor through the doorway, and the gentlemen would be offered a drink before he left. While he drank it his recent companion remained with him, not moving on to another guest before the first one left. Definitely, Longarm thought, a classy place.

Twice Longarm refused offers of company from the girls, but he did accept one of their cigars, which tasted as mellow as its appearance promised, and a tumbler of Maryland rye.

He was beginning to feel a little conspicuous—hell, he had paid for a roll in the hay and was just sitting here instead—when the one-legged man finally appeared in the doorway.

In the bright lights of the parlor, the man looked even more out of place than Longarm had suspected he would. His clothing came off a rack and could have stood some cleaning, and he was badly in need of a shave. Strange that he would be so readily accepted here, Longarm thought.

None of the other men in the room acknowledged his presence, the deputy saw, although several seemed to give him sidelong, disapproving glances.

This was interestinger and interestinger, Longarm thought wryly. It was especially so when the madam, Belle, hurried to join him and the girl who had just entertained him. The girl was dismissed, and the one-legged man crutched out of sight with Belle accompanying him. They disappeared toward the back of the house, not toward the front door.

A conference or a back door, Longarm wondered. Either way he could not follow, not without being entirely too obvious about it. He would have to settle for the next best thing.

"Miss."

"Sir?" The girl who had just come in with the one-legged man turned to answer the summons.

She stopped for a moment when she saw the tall, slim deputy, and smiled. "Yes, *indeed,* sir." She hurried over to him and draped herself over the arm of his chair.

"You're very pretty," Longarm said. He didn't even have to lie about it. She was young, probably not yet twenty, and was clear-eyed and pleasant looking. If he had passed her on the street Longarm would have mistaken her for some businessman's pampered daughter. He would never have guessed her to be in this profession. Which, he reflected, would have something to do with the outrageously high price they commanded here. "What is your name, girl?"

"Lenore." She giggled without any reason and simpered.

Well, he thought, that explained part of the reason she was in this line of work. He got the clear impression that Lenore was not burdened with more brain power than a scant minimum, in spite of her presentable appearance.

"Can I call you honeybun, honeybun?" She giggled again.

Longarm suppressed a desire to get the hell out of there and resigned himself to doing his duty. "Why don't you and I talk in private, Lenore?"

"Whatever you say, honeybun."

He winced.

Lenore led him through the wide doorway to a staircase Longarm had not been able to see from his chair. There were several closed-doors off the lower landing also. Behind one of those, or possibly long gone into a back alley by now, would be the one-legged man Longarm needed to know about. Damn it. He followed the girl up the stairs to a narrow second-floor hallway and on into a room that was small but furnished much better than his room back at the Buckhorn.

"Now, honeybun." Longarm barely had time to reach the bed and take a seat on it—there were no chairs provided—before Lenore was peeling herself out of her gown.

She stepped out of the gown with practiced speed and stood naked before him for his inspection.

In spite of himself, Longarm felt a stir of rising interest. The whore was built, he had to admit that. Her breasts were large but still had the uptilted firmness of youth, and her waist was tiny. Her hips had a delectably tantalizing swell, and her legs were long and shapely. Longarm swallowed hard. Only the realization that she had so recently been the recipient of the one-legged man's attentions kept him from being fully aroused by the sight of her body.

"Take your clothes off, honeybun, an' tell Lenore *exactly* what you want Lenore to do for you." She rolled her eyes and licked her lips and both hands suggestively roved through the light brown bush at the vee of her crotch. "French, honeybun, or in the ass? Both? We have *lots* of time, honeybun, and I'm gonna be *so* good for you, why, I'm gonna make your ears spin, my handsome honeybun." She gave him a wet-lipped smile and began to move toward him with her hips swaying and her big tits bouncing.

She was so damned lewdly exciting that Longarm might well have been tempted, but a gleam of reflected light caught his eye and brought his mind back to his business.

On the inside of her satin-smooth thigh there was a trickle of shiny fluid reflecting in the lamplight. The silly bitch hadn't bothered to completely clean herself after the last customer. It was more of a reminder than Longarm wanted of the one-legged man.

His face hardened at the same time as his interest went slack. "Sit down," he said coldly.

"What, honeybun?"

"Sit. No, damn it, keep your hand off me. That's better."

Lenore looked completely puzzled, unable to comprehend this peculiar desire of her gentleman caller. "But..."

"Shut up." Longarm was thinking rapidly. "I am here

on official business. Government business." He took his wallet out and showed it to her.

"But . . ."

"I told you to shut up."

"Yes, sir," she said meekly.

So far so good, he thought. He took a shot in the dark, feeling his way as he went by speaking with an icy edge to his voice. He wanted to put a scare into this dumb little whore. "You are a runaway," he said. "There is a warrant out for your arrest."

"But . . ."

"I told you to shut up."

"Yes, sir."

"That's better. You are a runaway, and Lenore is not your real name."

The girl's face crumpled with sudden dismay. She covered her face with her hands and began to cry. "I didn't . . . I didn't . . ."

Longarm had no idea what it was that she "didn't," and he could not afford to guess, or to have her realize that he could not know. He pulled her hands away from her face and coldly said, "I told you to shut up."

Her sniffling dried up immediately, and she sat up very straight with her shoulders squared and her hands in her lap. "Yes, sir." She looked straight ahead, her chin and underlip quivering only slightly.

She came, Longarm thought, either from some kind of institutional background or from a family with a military martinet at its head. One of those, he thought, but he could not afford to guess at which it might be.

"I am empowered to arrest you and take you back," he told her.

The girl began to cry again, but this time she kept her hands carefully in her lap and kept her face forward. Some son of a bitch had drilled a painfully rigid form of obedience into her, whatever her background.

She sat so rigidly that he was almost able to forget that

she was naked. Certainly she no longer seemed the least bit provocative or seductive.

He felt sorry for her but he could not let it show. Her lips trembled and the tears ran freely, but she did not look away from her eyes-front position and made no attempt to speak again.

"Prison is an ugly place," Longarm said coldly. "You have only the smallest chance to avoid it."

He could see her throat work as she swallowed. Her eyes started to cut toward him, then quickly straightened again. Longarm felt like a bastard for putting her through this, but he went on to the next step.

"There is a chance, only a chance, mind you, that I might be persuaded to forget I saw you here and leave you alone."

The girl's breath exploded outward in a wild sob, and before Longarm realized what she intended she had swung around and dropped to her knees in front of him.

"Anything, anything. I'll be good, oh, God, I'll be *so* good, you'll see, I promise, and. . ." She was fumbling with the buttons of his trousers, and he had some difficulty shooing her away from him.

"Not that," he said with ice in his voice.

She rocked back onto her heels, her tear-streaked face a mask of fear. Longarm was glad he *didn't* know what the poor thing had run from or what she might have had to do so she could get away.

She bent down and groveled, actually groveled, at his boots. "Anything. Anything at all. D'you want to beat me? Whip me? Anything. Just please don't. . ."

Longarm felt revolted, sickened. "I want information. Now." Somehow he managed 𝅘 ⟍ steel in his voice.

"Yes, sir. Anything." She kɴₑₗₜ ⟍ front of him, wringing her hands and crying.

"The man you were just with. Tell me about him."

She gave a loud sob of relief, and some of the tension in her dissipated. "Yes, sir, anything."

"The man with one leg," he prompted.

"Yes, sir. He didn't want that much, sir; likes us to lick his stump a while an' then a straight fuck. That's all, sir, I swear it."

Longarm made a face. "I don't care about the man's sex life, for crying out loud. I want to know who he is."

"His name?"

"For starters."

"Sid. His name's Sid, sir."

Longarm's interest quickened. Sidney Duck Bragg was the man he was looking for. One of them, anyway. This seemed almost too easy to be true.

It was.

"Mr. Sid, sir, I don't know his last name, he's a...a businessman here, sir."

"Business?" That didn't sound right, if this one-legged Sid was the powder monkey who was going to blow the safe or whatever in a train robbery.

"Business," the girl repeated. "You know."

Longarm shook his head. "Maybe I don't know."

"Mr. Sid, he's a regular here, sir." She glanced toward the closed and locked door of her room as if she expected someone to be lurking there, and when she spoke again she whispered to him. "Mr. Sid, he runs this place an' a couple others not so nice an' some cribs...."

Shit! Businessman, indeed. No wonder the man was welcome here. He *owned* the damn place. Longarm was so disappointed that he had come this far and done all this on a false lead that he almost missed the rest of what the frightened whore was saying.

"...an' some specialty places, one anyway, you know, for gentlemen that need something special so's they can get it up, like chains or animals or little girls an' like that."

"What?"

The girl looked nervously toward the door. "You—you ain't mad at me, are you? I mean, you wouldn't go back on your word an' send me back there or nothing, would you?"

Longarm forced himself to regain the hard, relentless expression of a blackmailer. "Tell me about this specialty stuff. And anything you know about Carl Deeb's connection with this Sid," he ordered.

The girl looked more frightened than ever when he mentioned Deeb's name. She seemed unwilling to say anything more.

But once she did begin to talk, she talked for quite a while. And Longarm felt sicker than ever when he finally left Sweet Belle's House of Joys.

Chapter 12

Every state and territory had the right to make its own laws. Longarm understood that and generally he approved of it. But there are some things that are just plain *wrong*. And this was among them.

He left the House of Joys feeling lousy about what he had done there and what he had heard there, but feeling also that the fifty-dollar fee he had paid Belle and, indirectly, the one-legged whoremaster called Sid had been money well spent. If Billy Vail balked at the amount coming out of Longarm's expenses, he would pay the damned fee himself and reimburse the government out of his own slim bank account.

At the moment he did not care at all either that this one-legged man had turned out to be the wrong suspect.

Now Longarm wanted to get the son of a bitch stopped.

He headed first from the Crystal Palace, stopping at every saloon and gaming house along the way to poke his head inside and look for the man he wanted. He had had no luck by the time he reached the Palace, so he strode rapidly to the bar and beckoned Jake Jacobs to join him. The bartender reached for a mug but stopped the motion when he saw Longarm's face. He hurried down to Longarm's end of the bar.

"What is it, Marshal?" he asked.

"I'm looking for Deputy Hank Bigelow," Longarm said.

"Sounds like you want him in a hurry."

"I do."

"Hank don't much like to be disturbed when he's off duty, but..."

"He won't mind this." Longarm hoped and believed he was telling the truth there.

"All right. But you won't likely find Hank doing any carousing. He's a family man, Hank is. Your best bet is to look in at his house."

"Where?"

"It's... just a minute, Marshal, 'cause I ain't for sure." Jacobs called another man over from the end of the bar and had a brief, whispered conversation with him. The man joined Longarm and, reluctantly, it seemed, gave him directions to the Bigelow home.

"I appreciate this, Jake," said Longarm.

"Anything I can do, Marshal. Is... uh... there any possibility of getting a piece of reward money out of this?"

"Not that I know of." Longarm paused, then smiled. "But I noticed you gave the help before you asked the question. Thanks again, friend."

"Any time."

Longarm left the ornate saloon and turned north. According to the directions it was about half a mile to Bigelow's house, but it would be quicker to walk it than to find a horse or a rig for hire at this hour. It was already something into the wee hours, and even Virginia City was not *that* wide open.

He found the house without delay, but as he had expected it was closed up and darkened. "Sorry, old son," Longarm muttered as he climbed the steps to the front door, "looks like you lose some sleep tonight."

He banged on the door, and after several minutes a gleam of yellow light showed through the curtained windows flanking the front door.

"Yes?" It was a woman's voice, and it was a plump, pretty woman with a cloak thrown over her nightdress who opened the door for him.

Longarm swept his Stetson off. "Sorry to disturb you, ma'am, but I believe this is the Bigelow house?"

"Yes."

"I need to see Hank, Mrs. Bigelow."

"Just a moment then." She took the precaution of closing and bolting the door again before she went to fetch her husband. Longarm didn't mind; Mrs. Bigelow would not know him from Adam's off ox and in a place as ornery as most mining camps were a body could not be too careful.

"This better be . . . Oh, it's you." Bigelow's expression changed quickly from annoyance to interest when he saw who the midnight caller was. "Come in."

"No, I think maybe you'd better come out, Hank. With a badge and a gun if you wouldn't mind."

The local deputy brightened. "You spotted your man already?"

Longarm shook his head. "Something else. And as far as I know, Hank, nobody's bothered to write any federal law on this subject, so I'll have to be the informant and you handle any arresting that's to be done."

Bigelow looked puzzled, but he did not waste any time asking for explanations. He let the federal man into his parlor and disappeared to get his clothing. While he was gone Mrs. Bigelow came out and offered to make coffee.

"When we get back that would be real nice, ma'am," Longarm said, "but not right now." She left him alone in the parlor with a small lamp to keep him company.

While he waited Longarm looked around the tiny room in the very small house that Hank Bigelow could afford on the salary of a county deputy. It wasn't much, but it was a home. And Bigelow had a wife, maybe kids as well, to keep him company in it. Longarm did not envy the man. He had chosen his way of life with his eyes open and his decisions consciously made. Still, he had to admire a man with the staying qualities that a family man had to have. It was something Custis Long was not sure he could manage himself.

"I'm ready," Bigelow said from the hallway.

"Do you keep horses here, Hank?"

"One. For official use. He'll pull a rig when need be, if that will help."

"I reckon. What about other men handy?"

It was Hank Bigelow's turn to shake his head. "I told you there are some other good boys on the county payroll, but they're all assigned out in the county, and it's a pretty fair-sized piece of territory. I could get 'em in here by tomorrow evening, maybe. In town right now there's just me an' the sheriff an' Carl Deeb. Do you want me to fetch them out?"

Longarm made a face. "A little while ago, Hank, I saw Deeb take a payoff about this thing. We sure can't use him. And I don't know that I'd want the sheriff notified either until it's too late."

Bigelow went pale. "I don't like the son of a bitch, Longarm, but taking hush money, well . . ."

"I understand. It's an ugly thing I'm saying, Hank. I'm sorry."

"Tell me about it."

"While we hitch that horse of yours to something that will roll."

Ten minutes later they were on the road south. Hank Bigelow's face was set in a hard expression. "If you're right, Longarm . . ."

"My informant sure believed it."

"Bastards!"

"I know."

"I got two little girls of my own, Longarm. Did you know that?"

102

Longarm shook his head.

"Well, I do. Amy is four. Becky's not quite two yet. I keep thinking..."

"Don't."

The deputy sighed. "I expect you're right. But it ain't easy to do, you know."

"Tell me about it."

"You got any kids?"

"No."

"Pity," Bigelow said. He sounded as if he meant it.

Maybe it was a pity, too, Longarm thought. But not tonight.

Bigelow stopped briefly at the courthouse and used his ring of keys to get into the sheriff's office. He came back with a pair of ten-gauge double-barrelled shotguns with their barrels cut short and a box of Number Two shot shells that he broke open on the seat between them. "Fill your pockets, Longarm." He handed him one of the scatterguns. Both men loaded their blunt, deadly persuaders.

"I'm assuming," Longarm said, "that we've got a violation of the law here."

Bigelow flashed a brief, tight grin. "So'm I."

"You don't know?"

"I *think* it is. Is that good enough?"

"Hell, yes."

Hank Bigelow snapped his buggy whip over the back of his indignant saddle gelding, and the light rig lurched forward.

The place looked like any other derelict equipment shed except for a low-trimmed lantern that burned near the door. The shack was scarcely big enough to turn around in but, like so many others in the area, it covered the mouth of an abandoned mine tunnel where the drifts had paid out.

Now, he understood, the old tunnel was being put to other uses.

A hundred yards or so below reaching the shack they

had passed a number of tethered horses and parked buggies, left there in the dark where they would not draw attention to the shack. Judging from that, the place seemed to be well attended. Longarm scowled when he thought about the men who had come here, and if any of them could have seen him they would have been chilled marrow-deep.

"Ready, Longarm?" Bigelow asked.

"Uh-huh."

"You got any cuffs on you?"

"No, damn it. They're back in my hotel room."

"I brought some, but after lookin' at that crowd of animals I don't know that I brought enough." Bigelow sighed. "If I know anything about the way things go around here, Longarm, I'd say that we only want to cuff the people runnin' this place, anyhow. The customers we'll have to let walk."

Longarm made a face, but he nodded. "It's your show, Deputy. I'm just here as a concerned citizen, so to speak."

"Right. Well . . . let's do it."

They climbed down out of Bigelow's buggy, and Longarm heard the soft, rolling snick of oiled metal on metal as the hammers of Hank's scattergun were earred back. Longarm draped his thumb over the hammers of his own shotgun and walked forward with the tubes of the ugly weapon dangling deceptively low. If he needed the gun, though, he could get it into action as quickly as his own familiar Colt.

Bigelow stopped at the leather-hung door of the shack and knocked softly.

"Yo." The sound of chair legs and boots hitting the floor came through the door, and a moment later it was opened by a huge man who peered out at them. "What the he—" The question was cut short by the introduction of Hank Bigelow's shotgun muzzles pressing up against the shelf of the man's jaw. The fellow was big enough to handle a roomful of rowdies, but the feel of that cold steel against his throat stopped him dead still and deadly pale.

Holding the shotgun in one hand with his finger curled

tight against the front trigger, Bigelow fished in his pockets and shook out a pair of handcuffs. Without a word he handed the cuffs to Longarm, who applied them to the bouncer with the fellow's arms wrapped around a support timber next to the tunnel mouth at the back of the small shack. Bigelow removed the shotgun from its nest in the big man's throat.

"I think," Hank said. "if we gag this son of a bitch he might still be able to make some noise."

"Could be," Longarm agreed.

Bigelow slashed at the back of the man's head with the butt of his shotgun, and the fellow crumpled to the floor. "I don't reckon he'll make much noise now."

"Go easy, Hank. You might've killed him," Longarm said.

"Might have at that." Bigelow did not sound particularly distressed by the thought.

"Better to try 'em before the execution, Hank," Longarm said softly.

The quick anger in Bigelow's expression faltered. More calmly he said, "You're right, Longarm. I reckon I'll do my fuckin' duty here if it makes me puke."

"Good." Longarm gave him a smile.

A row of lamps hung on spikes driven into the tunnel walls led deep into the hillside. From somewhere far down the tunnel they could hear an anguished scream and then the rising lament of several crying children. Bigelow's face tightened again.

"Easy, Hank."

The deputy took a deep breath. "Sure."

"I mean it, Hank. I don't want to have to take you out, too."

"I'm tryin', man."

"Let's go, then."

Shotguns ready, they edged forward along the well lighted tunnel. The sounds of loud wailing continued to sweep up the tunnel to greet them.

Chapter 13

The madam of the weird brothel was in a short drift tunnel to the left of the main tunnel about seventy-five yards in. The drift had been widened somewhat to serve as a parlor of sorts and was furnished now with rugs, sofas, and lamps. The number of lamps in use, though, could not begin to light the gaping, black mouth of a stope that rose overhead.

The madam was not what Longarm would have expected. He had fully, if unrealistically, expected something resembling a cackling witch in a child's fairy-tale book. Instead the woman was reasonably presentable in a dusty gown and with a liberal sprinkling of silver in her otherwise dark hair. She was heavy and matronly and not at all what Longarm would have recognized as the mistress of a place like this.

When the two men stepped into the entrance to the drift she was in the process of handing over a thin girl of no more than eight to a portly and very well-dressed gentleman. The child was crying. The man already had his tie undone and the buttons of his vest unfastened. His face was flushed with eagerness.

Their tableau was interrupted, stopped cold as if in a

photograph, by the arrival of the two officers. Their attention was commanded by Hank Bigelow's pointing shotgun, and in less than the space of a second each of the three had eyes as wide as the twin mouths of the ten-gauge scattergun.

Bigelow broke the silence first. He nodded to the gentleman and said, "Sir."

The man swallowed heavily.

"You better leave, sir," the deputy said.

The man gulped and nodded vigorously. He scurried out of the drift past Longarm, who was hanging back to make sure no one went by them in the main tunnel, and was already fumbling with his necktie before he reached the fresh night air outside.

The madam managed for a fleeting second to look indignant at this intrusion. "You have no right . . ." She took another look at the faces of the two men, and her voice died.

"Step over there against the wall, honey," Bigelow said softly to the little girl.

The child gave the madam a worried look, then did as she was told.

"Easy, Hank," Longarm murmured. "Don't shoot the bitch. She ain't worth losing your badge over." It took no great amount of sensitivity to see that Bigelow was having trouble controlling himself. "I'd have to put it in my report, Hank. You do what you got to, but I'd have to write it down."

Bigelow nodded. He was trembling, but he laid the shotgun aside on a low table and took out a pair of handcuffs.

"On the other hand, Hank, we don't want this woman to make any noise. And I think I'd better check the main tunnel to see we're left alone." Longarm turned away and stared pointedly down the length of the tunnel toward where all the crying was coming from.

Behind him he heard a dull, moist sound, and when he turned back the madam was unconscious on the floor. Still, under oath in a court of law he could not have testified that

107

he had seen anything happen there, not even if he wanted to in the worst way. 🔹

"What about the kid, Hank?"

Bigelow paused and looked at the child. "You wait right there, honey. You're going to be all right now. Everything's going to be fine. I want you to wait where you are an' we'll be back for you in a few minutes."

The child stared at him with wide eyes, and after a moment she nodded. She went to one of the sofas and perched stiffly on the forward edge of it with her hands folded primly in her lap. Longarm got the impression she was well used to unquestioning obedience, regardless of what the order might be. He doubted, though, that she could believe that *anything* was going to be all right, ever again.

"Come on, Hank. We have work to do."

The walk down the length of the tunnel was a nightmare that Longarm suspected he would relive in his sleep for a long time to come. Each new drift held its own new brand of depravity. Several had been set up as dungeons, with chains spiked into solid rock and manacles welded to their free ends. Whips and racks were in abundance. In a few light bamboo fishing rods had been substituted for the whips. Even with their ferrules removed they would cut flesh as effectively as any knife, as was demonstrated on the flesh of a young woman or girl—it was impossible for them to tell which—who had been receiving the attentions of a sweating, naked, red-faced man when Longarm and Bigelow arrived. That one, customer or not, was cuffed to the same manacles that had so recently held the object of his distorted "affections."

Farther back in the tunnel, it got worse. They found a drift, with a bolted door fitted, where the victims were kept.

Hank Bigelow stopped there to splatter the walls with what remained of his dinner.

Some of the children were no older than his, and there were boys as well as girls among them.

108

There was no one in the room to attend them or minister to their hurts. They lay with blank, uncaring eyes on narrow cots with straw ticks, waiting for whatever would be done to them next.

Longarm was glad there was no adult employee of the place present then. Bigelow would have killed the person on the spot. And Longarm was not so damn sure that he might not have helped.

They gave a few words of assurance to a girl who seemed to be the oldest and the strongest of the poor lot and left, leaving the door open.

"I can't believe we've come this far without a dustup," Longarm said, trying to take Bigelow's thoughts away from what they were seeing at every fresh turn and twist of the long tunnel.

His answer was a low, snarling grunt. It was plain that Hank Bigelow would have been happier if there *had* been trouble to deal with.

Longarm had spoken too soon. He knew it as soon as they stepped into the next drift.

The man who occupied the area was a handsome, moustached fellow in his thirties or younger. He was naked except for a wide belt of thick, black leather studded heavily with short spikes, but Longarm got the distinct impression that had the man been clothed he would have been dressed in fashionable, carefully tailored garments, that he usually presented himself to the world as a man of power and influence . . . and that he had both at his disposal when he chose to use them.

The man was crouching over a hard oak table that was crisscrossed with lengths of light chain. Held down by the chain, unable to escape, was a young child—boy or girl, it was impossible to see at the moment—with glazed, agonized eyes bulging under curly ringlets of soft blonde hair. The child was screaming horribly from the intrusions into its tiny body.

Longarm and Bigelow slipped inside the curtained entrance to the drift and saw at a glance what was being done there. Longarm heard a strangled gurgle of sound from his partner, and he turned quickly to stare down the tunnel, away from the room and its depraved occupant and tiny victim.

The roaring bellow of a ten-gauge shotgun sounded, magnified even beyond its normal intensity by the closeness of the hard rock walls of the tunnel, and a heavy shower of dust and dirt rained down from the tunnel ceiling and walls.

The roar rolled down the tunnel and echoed back to them. Longarm was only faintly conscious of that, because the concussion of the large-bore blast had dulled his hearing, and he was coughing and choking from the dust that was now thick in the atmosphere within the old mine.

Dimly he could hear Hank Bigelow coughing too.

"Bastard!" Bigelow yelled between coughs. "Went for something in that pile o' clothes over there. Gun, prob'ly."

Longarm said nothing.

Damn them, he thought. *Lord, damn them each and every one. Damn them.*

He had known before he turned his head, so he could not see, that this time Bigelow was sure to shoot. And he knew equally well that there would not be anything in Custis Long's official report to dispute whatever claim Hank Bigelow might want to make in the matter.

Damn them, Longarm thought. *There are some duties that go beyond the ones a man carries when he pins on a badge.*

He had given himself an out, shaky as it was, and he was going to use it.

But, damn it, Bigelow was going to have to carry a burden after this that Longarm might have shared and was not.

In spite of the cold logic of badge and duty, Longarm was not sure he had done the right thing by allowing Bigelow to carry it alone.

Longarm felt sick. His ears still ringing and buzzing from the shock of the too closely confined shotgun blast, he closed his eyes and leaned against the solid presence of the rock wall at his side. His gut felt queasy, and he gulped in air and dust as he stood like that.

It was only some sixth sense or barely heard impression of sound that saved him.

Without consciously acknowledging whatever warning it was that reached him, through whatever sense it might have been, Longarm's eyes snapped back open, and his right hand swept the shotgun to waist level.

There was a man running toward him. A man with a gun in his hand.

Visibility was poor through the dust that filled the stale air of the mine, but the lamplight from the wall brackets clearly showed the man's form and the gleam of light on the steel of a revolver that was rising to aim toward Longarm's chest.

Longarm tripped the front trigger of the awesome weapon in his hand, and once again the intensity of the explosion dwarfed all other senses, driving through flesh as easily as air and surrounding Longarm with an impression of noise so great it had an almost tangible presence.

The gun bucked in his hand so hard his wrist hurt, and he almost lost his grip on the shotgun.

Not that he needed it.

A few yards further down the tunnel, the man who had been aiming the revolver was now a torn pile of bloody scraps assembled in the shape of a human figure. The heavy charge of shot had done its awful work and nearly torn the man apart.

Longarm blinked and tried to concentrate on watching through what was now an almost solid curtain of drifting dust caused by that second explosion.

He felt a hand touch his shoulder, although he had heard no one approach, and he whirled at the ready.

111

If he had had a pistol in his hand instead of the longer shotgun he probably would have cut down Hank Bigelow, too. Only Bigelow's closeness gave Longarm a chance to recognize the deputy before he could bring the scattergun to bear.

"It's you," Longarm tried to say. He was not positive that the words came out, becasue if they did he could not hear them. He could not even hear his own voice in the aftermath of the powerful explosion. Longarm worked his mouth and jaw and tried again, but he still could not hear.

He saw Bigelow's mouth move, but whether there was sound or not Longarm could not tell. He shrugged and pointed to his ears, shaking his head. Bigelow nodded.

The local deputy disappeared back into the drift for a moment. Longarm did not have to look in there to know what the sight would be. There was a similar spectacle on the floor out here in the tunnel. He did not particularly want to see another.

When Bigelow came out again he was carrying in his arms a small, plump figure that looked like it had been painted red.

Longarm's eyes widened, but Bigelow quickly gestured that the child was all right. The pellets had ripped into its tormenter, but at such close range the kid had not been touched. The blood had all apparently come from the man Bigelow shot.

The two went on through the remainder of the tunnel, but by now they were almost immune to the sights that came before them. And they no longer found any customers in the act of enjoying their peculiar pleasures. The gunshots had guaranteed that.

The few more men they found were all fully dressed, doing their level best to pretend that they were alone in their hired chambers.

Longarm had had to take the lead for that last part of the raid. Hank Bigelow walked behind with his shotgun in one hand and the blood-spattered child clutched tightly to him with the other. He seemed adamant that he would not relinquish the child, even when Longarm tried to put the youngster into the care of a twelve- or thirteen-year-old girl they freed from a whipping post. Bigelow would only shake his head and hold the child tighter.

At length they reached the end of the tunnel, and Longarm stopped there to lean against the end wall and draw in the much cleaner air here. He shot his jaw and rubbed at his ears.

"Can you hear me?" Bigelow was asking.

"Some." Longarm was pleased. This time he could hear his own voice. That was a relief. A deaf man would have a hell of a time trying to pass muster as a federal officer, no matter how good he was otherwise.

"We got to go, Longarm," Bigelow said. "All them customers are out by now an' I know at least two of 'em that will be heading straight for the county judge's house. We got to get our prisoners back before things get too confused in town."

Longarm nodded. He felt more exhausted, more utterly soul-weary, than he could ever remember being before.

His hand sagged down and straightened, and he let the sawed-off shotgun clatter unheeded to the rock floor of the old tunnel. It was county property, and he really did not give a damn about it. He felt just too tired to carry the damn thing any more.

They turned and, Bigelow still carrying the small child, started back up the tunnel to collect their two prisoners and decide what they should do about the youngsters who had been held here.

That, too, would be the county's problem, but Longarm thought it was unlikely all of them could ever be reunited with their proper families.

Jesus, he thought, some of them were too young to *know* who their own families were.

Longarm clumped wearily up the tunnel with Bigelow and the child at his heels.

"Marshal?"

He stopped and turned, thinking it odd that Hank Bigelow would be addressing him that way after what they had just been through together.

They had just passed the body of the man Longarm had shot. Bigelow was standing over the ragged, bloody form, looking down at the dead man's face.

"Yeah, Hank?"

"Why didn't you tell me?"

"Tell you what, Hank?"

Bigelow pointed with the barrels of his shotgun. Longarm stepped forward. He looked down and swore.

"I didn't know," he said. "The dust was so thick, I never got a good look at him. Didn't want a look afterward, neither, if the truth be known."

Bigelow nodded and let out a long sigh. "For the best anyhow, maybe."

"Maybe."

The dead man on the tunnel floor was Carl Deeb.

"No wonder he never told on them," said Bigelow.

"Yeah." Longarm turned and began to walk slowly out of the mine. He was awfully tired, and there was so much work yet to be done.

Damn them, Longarm thought.

Especially the ones who walked away. Handcuffs and cell bars would contain only the few who could be charged. The others, the bastards who created the demand for these awful services, were still free to prey on others.

The worst part of it, Longarm thought, was that those men would almost certainly do so. Even more carefully in the future than they had before, to be sure; but their tastes would not change, and there was nothing that a simple deputy marshal could think of that would make them change.

There were times, he thought, when a man could wish

for a whole lot more power than a badge and an oath of office gave him.

He sighed and stumbled and wished for a tall glass of Maryland rye to settle his nerves and soothe his stomach.

He brightened a little. *Hell,* he thought, *at least there are some wishes in life that can be met.*

Chapter 14

"Are you all right, Custis?" Millicent looked very small and rather frightened when she met him at the door of the hotel room. She had a sheet draped around her, and one bare shoulder peeked fetchingly out of the folds of cloth. It had come daylight long since, but she looked as if she had just awakened at his knock.

"I'm fine," Longarm assured her.

"You look tired."

"Uh-huh."

"I tried to wait up for you. I guess I fell asleep, though. You aren't mad, are you?"

"Of course not." He shut and locked the door behind him, and Millicent gave him an impish grin. She let the sheet fall away to confirm the promise of that bare shoulder. She was bare all over.

Longarm held her and kissed her, but he felt awkward and wooden with her in his arms. After the night he had just spent, sex was the furthest thing from his mind.

"You're *sure* you are all right?"

"Just tired, Milly."

She helped him out of his clothes and guided him to the bed, still warm from her use. She plumped the pillow for him and tucked him under the covers. Only when Longarm was relaxed and comfortable, his eyes closed and his over-worked thoughts slipping toward sleep, did Millicent crawl in to lie quietly beside him.

Longarm woke to a warm, gentle touch. He was fully erect before he came awake, and he could feel a slow, soft stroking repeating itself up and down the length of his shaft.

For a moment he lay basking in the delightful sensation.

Then memories of the night before rocked him, and his thoughts were flooded by the sights and sounds and horrors of the mine tunnel. He went suddenly and completely limp.

"Custis?"

"It's all right, Milly."

She bent to him again and took him into her mouth. She had no touble at all drawing all of him into herself in his flaccid state.

He felt what she was doing. It even felt very good to him still. But it did nothing to regain his erection. He kept thinking about the tunnel.

Millicent released him and sat up. Her face twisted. She was trying to smile bravely, but she seemed to be too near tears to make the would-be smile anything more than a ghastly imitation of what it was intended to be.

"I'm sorry," he said.

"Oh, it's . . . all right. I understand."

"Do you?"

"Sure, I . . ." She turned her head away, not looking him in the eye. "I have no claim to you, Custis. You're free to spend your time with anyone you wish, and you have a perfect right to be exhausted now." She raised a hand and scrubbed at her eyes as if she was rubbing sleep out of them. She absolutely was *not* crying, her gesture seemed to say.

"Spend time with . . . oh. You think I was with some other woman last night."

"You don't have to explain anything to me, Custis. Truly you don't. Why, I . . ."

"Hush. Hush now, Milly." He shushed her with a finger pressed against her lips. He followed that with a kiss. In spite of what she was thinking about him, she responded gladly to his embrace.

"There's something I ought to tell you, Millicent. I want to tell you all about last night. And why I didn't come back here to be with you. And why I reacted—or didn't react— the way I did a minute ago. Hush now. Don't say it."

"All right." She lay back beside him. She looked worried about what she was going to hear, but she accepted his wish in the matter and was silent then.

"It isn't at all what you think, Milly," Longarm said.

He paused for several long moments. Then he began, slowly at first, to talk. He told her the whole story.

"So I am not exactly popular in some quarters here, Millicent," he finished. "And those sons of bitches are not high on my list either, as a matter of fact. But, ugly as it is, that's what happened last night. I'm sorry you had to listen to it. I just wanted you to understand. I hope you do."

Millicent was crying. "Oh, Custis, I'm so sorry you had to go through all that, you and Deputy Bigelow. But I'm so proud of you both for doing what you did." She sat up and dried her eyes, then left the bed and stood at its side. "Look at me, please, Custis."

"What?"

"Look at me. Look at my body."

He turned his head and did as she asked. What he saw was lovely, a ripe, full, entirely desirable woman's body.

Millicent cupped her breasts in her hands and ran her palms down across the flat plane of her stomach to the thatch of curling hair above her sex. She touched herself lightly and parted the lips of her vagina for him to see.

She smiled. "Hey, that feels *good*. I've never done that before. I like it."

Longarm laughed. "Good for you."

"Seriously now, Custis. What do you see when you look at my body?"

"You know the answer to that."

"Tell me."

"All right. I see one very damned good looking woman when I look at your body, Millicent. I see a woman any man in his right mind would want."

"Truly?"

"Of course."

"The key word there, Custis, is 'woman.' I'm all grown up. And I am *not* allowing you to *use* my body, Custis. I *want* you. It isn't something for you to *take*, dear. It is something I am offering to *give* you. Making love with you is something *I* want, too. It isn't something just for you to enjoy. It's for me, too. Do you understand what I'm trying to tell you, Custis?"

"Sure, but..."

"No 'but' about it, dear. Think about what I just said. No, damn it, really *think* about it. I'm not in any hurry. You do some genuine thinking about it while I go brush my hair. But don't go anyplace. I'll be back." She turned and crossed the room to the bureau with its small, cracked mirror hung on the wall over it. She dug in her purse for a hairbrush and began brushing her long, unpinned hair.

When she was done and she did return she said nothing to Longarm. She pulled the covers back off the bed to expose the full, hard-muscled length of his body.

Millicent gave him a warm smile and blew him a kiss, but it was at his waist that she knelt to bend over him.

Her hair spilled down over his scrotum, lightly teasing his balls as she leaned closer and ran the tip of her tongue over him. In spite of himself Longarm felt a stir of interest.

Millicent must have noticed the faint thickening of his shaft, because she smiled. She took him into her mouth, and now he was definitely growing hard. His cock lengthened as it became firmer, and soon she had to back off and allow some of him to escape to keep from choking.

Millicent sighed and bent herself happily to the task of pleasing him.

"Smart-ass woman," Longarm muttered.

"What?"

"Nothing."

She released him and looked up. "What did you say?"

He grinned at her. "Not a damn thing, woman. Now get back to what you were doing before you get me riled."

"Yes, sir, yes, indeed, sir." She flashed him a smile and did as she was told.

Longarm stifled a yawn and finished buttoning his vest. He strung his watch chain across his flat stomach and tucked the little brass derringer into its accustomed place, then settled his gunbelt comfortably around his hips, taking care to make sure the Colt rode precisely where it ought to.

"It certainly takes you long enough to get dressed," Millicent said with a smile.

"You had a head start, as I recall."

She gave him another satisfied smile. "I had always heard that one good woman could outlast a dozen men. Now I am ready to believe it."

"I was right," Longarm said. "You're a smart-ass woman, Millicent."

She stuck her tongue out at him.

He grinned. "Careful with that thing. It's a dangerous weapon in the right quarters."

"Are you ready to prove that, buster?"

"Give a man some rest, will you?"

"You prove my point, sir, about man being the weaker sex."

Longarm ignored that and said, "Personally, now that I've had my way with you, I'm ready for some breakfast."

Millicent laughed and looked out the window toward the twilit evening sky. "If you go down asking for breakfast, dear, you are going to raise eyebrows. You worked through

120

breakfast and slept your way through lunch." She giggled. "Almost screwed your way past dinner, too."

Oh, she was in fine fettle now, he thought. Give some women a proper loving and they get so full of themselves they just can't stand it.

Still, that kind of vigorous exercise can make a man hungry as a wolverine in springtime. And if she had her mouth full of steak she was almost certain to shut up. "Come on, woman, before you get yourself into trouble that you can't handle."

Millicent shot her hips forward and gave him a lewd wink. "I can handle it, buster."

"Okay, but I'm leaving." He opened the door.

She gave out a little squeal and hurried after him.

Chapter 15

"Mind if I join you?"

"Of course not." Longarm made the introductions. "Millicent, this is Hank Bigelow. Hank, this is Miss Cater."

The deputy took his hat off. "Miss."

"My pleasure, Mr. Bigelow."

They were in the lobby of the Buckhorn. Longarm was having a cheroot and a heavy jolt of Maryland rye. Millicent had a barely touched glass of champagne beside her.

"What would you like, Hank?" Longarm asked.

Bigelow gave him a wan smile. "A chance to get off my feet would be nice."

"Sit down, man. Can I get you anything else?"

Bigelow shook his head. "Not yet. This has been a long day and promises to be just as long an evening. I'll sure be glad to get home tonight." He smiled. "An' you, Longarm, don't you be expecting a cheerful welcome the next time you come calling at my door. I've only been home long enough since to change my clothes and get back down to the courthouse. You started hell a-rolling in this town, Longarm. Beggin' your pardon, miss."

Millicent pretended not to have heard the inappropriate word. That was something Longarm rather admired about ladies. The genuine article—which Millicent certainly seemed to be—could have a man's pecker in her mouth one minute, and the very next minute butter wouldn't melt in that self-same mouth. Intriguing, he thought, and admirable in its own odd way.

"Rough day, huh?" he asked.

"You bet." Hank sighed. "Let me tell you, federal man, you got the easy side of this badge-carryin' life. Those federal judges you deal with, they don't have to care what ol' Harve down at the general mercantile thinks about their decisions. Us poor bastards out in the counties, we got to put up with the judges that don't know—" He glanced toward Millicent and moderated his choice of words on her behalf. "Hardly nothing about the law an' less about wearing backbones."

Longarm had his own opinions about certain political appointees who held federal judicial seats, but this did not seem like the time or the company for spinning his own sad tales. That was better held within unless he was alone with Billy Vail in the marshal's closed office, the proper time for letting off steam. "Can you handle it, Hank?" he asked sympathetically.

"Oh, I'm handling it, I reckon. I won't say it's been real easy, but I'm handling it." He rubbed the heel of his hand over his tense neck muscles. "I don't suppose you've heard yet about the sheriff?"

"He wasn't . . ."

"No. Least, I don't suppose so. His pet deputy getting shot like that, though, kinda took the heart out of the bastard. Excuse me, miss."

Millicent gave him a polite nod and took a dainty sip from her glass, as if she hadn't heard a thing that needed excusing. Longarm knew damn well from the way she was sitting, jaw set and body canted just the least bit toward the two men, that she was hanging on every word Hank Bigelow uttered.

"What happened," Hank said, "was that Sheriff D. K. Randolph went and resigned from office late this morning."

"You know what that likely means, then."

Bigelow nodded glumly. "Looks to me, an' to everybody else too, I expect, that Deke has been getting part of the take. 'Specially since Deeb likely would of took his payoff in trade if it was just him. Finding him there like that, well, it kinda looks like Deke had to be filling his pockets outa the same trough."

"I hope nobody ever promised you this was gonna be an easy line of work, Hank," said Longarm.

"No, but nobody ever said it was gonna be this tough, neither."

"Who's minding the store until they can have a special election, then? I'd think that could have an effect on how hard the case is pushed."

"Well, I guess I am."

"Sheriff?"

"Acting sheriff, anyhow."

Longarm grinned. "They have a good man in the job, Sheriff. You'll do just fine. If you take my advice about it, you'll stand for election, too."

"I guess there's been some folks have mentioned that possibility today, federal man."

"I'm glad for you, Hank. And for your family—with all due apologies to your wife."

Bigelow smiled. "That's fine, just so long as you don't expect to hear her forgiving *you.*" He rubbed his neck again. "Look, Longarm, I didn't come over here just to tell you things've been lousy today. 'Cause they haven't. Not all the time.

"What I'm saying is, there's an awful lot of good folks in Virginia City. They don't like that sort of thing any better than you and me do. And they're grateful to you for helping clean up a bad situation."

"Most towns are like that, Hank. The good outnumber the bad; they're just quieter about it."

"Yeah. Well, there's even been some real hardcases looking for a way to tell you they appreciate what you done last night, Longarm. So what I done was, I put the word out to a few of them—you know the kind I mean, I expect, on the edge of the law or somewhere past it, but with some decency in them, too—anyway, I put the word out that it would maybe help you if you was to locate this Professor fella and his one-legged powder monkey and them." He paused and looked Longarm in the eye. "These are the kind of boys, Longarm, that would of heard if there was anything, I mean *any* dang thing, to it."

"And?"

"Nothing, my friend. Not a whisper. I even talked to one fella who admitted to having worked with this Duck Bragg in the past. He says if there was anything in the wind here, he's the first one Bragg would of come to to join in on the deal. They parted on good terms, you see, and have made some good hauls together, which he adds he will never admit to in a court of law if I was to call him on it. But in private, he says it's the natural truth and he'd swear to it between him and me. I believe him, Longarm."

Longarm shook his head. "I sure don't understand this, Hank."

"I'd be willing to swear the man was being straight with me."

"That's not what I'm doubting, Hank. Believe me, I know how it can be with a man who's tipping you. You get the feel soon enough if he's trying to fool you. No— what I can't figure is why an informant would run all the way to Cheyenne to spill this an' go to the trouble of getting himself killed over it, yet still prove out as wrong as this looks to be. That's what is throwing me."

"I wish I could help you, Longarm, I really do."

Longarm smiled. "You have, Hank. You've done more in one afternoon than I could've accomplished alone in the

125

next month. By which time, damn it, this robbery should have already taken place."

Bigelow frowned. "That's something else I can't figure about your case, Longarm. I mean, we ship out of here all the time, sure. But what kind of fool is gonna rob a silver train, for cryin' out loud? It would take another whole train just to haul the stuff away. Enough to make it worthwhile, anyhow. Silver is valuable stuff, but it sure is bulky. Why, I doubt a man could buy enough mules this side of Missoura to carry the amount that this robbery is s'posed to be for."

Longarm shook his head. "It's supposed to be gold, Hank, not silver. But even so there'd be a lot of it, true. Bulky even if it's concentrated but not to the refinery yet."

"Gold! From here? Hell, Longarm we don't ship gold outa Virginia City but once, maybe twice a year. Not to amount to anything, we don't. Silver is what makes the Comstock spin, my friend. The gold that started the strike was skimmed off years ago."

"Gold, silver, I . . . Do you know what I did, Hank? I forgot to pay *attention*, that's what I did. Got so carried away thinking about one piece of information that I forgot to really pay attention to the rest. Are you *sure*, about the gold, I mean?"

Bigelow gave him a dirty look. "This is my town, Marshal. And if there was to be any kind of big gold shipment planned I would for sure know about it way in advance. I can absolutely promise you there isn't one in the works out of Virginia City, my friend. Not any time in the next two, three months, there won't be."

Longarm shook his head. "And the Professor and his boys absolutely haven't been seen around here."

"That's the word I get from the people who ought to know," Hank agreed.

"Damn." Longarm stood.

"Where are you off to?"

"Back to the beginning. Or close to it, anyway. I got to talk to Kyle Lewis back in Cheyenne and take a fresh start on this. There's something—I don't know what, but something—that I've missed in my hurry to get out here and catch the Professor. I got to find out whatever that something is and correct it before it's too late."

Acting Sheriff Bigelow gave him a look of warning. "You know what will happen if we're both wrong, Longarm, and your Professor fellow pulls off a big robbery while you're away from where you were sent."

Longarm grinned. "Sure I know, Hank. I'd be chewed down to a bloody nub an' then I'd be coming back here looking for work. Right?"

"I guess you do know, at that."

"Are you coming, Millicent?" Longarm asked.

"What?"

"Stay here if you'd rather. Come to think of it, that might be safer for you than coming with me. But I did promise you the story. I'll stick to that if you want."

She was on her feet quickly. "I'm not letting this story get away from me. Uh-uh."

Longarm shook hands with Hank Bigelow. "Good luck to you, Sheriff. If you need me for the trial or anything . . ."

"I know how to reach you." Hank smiled. "Just remember. You don't have to have any official excuses to come back here. You're welcome in my town or in my home any time, Longarm." The smile became a grin. "Soon as my better half cools down, that is."

Longarm hurried away. There was a late train they could still catch. He wondered if he should wire Billy Vail about this minor change of location—minor being a thousand miles or thereabouts—or if he should leave the marshal happy in his ignorance of just how poorly this case was going.

Chapter 16

They reached Cheyenne in the normal state of post-travel weariness, but even so Longarm did not want to take a hotel room immediately. If he learned anything of interest from Kyle Lewis, he knew, they might have to turn right around and speed back to Virginia City as quickly as the rails could get them there, and sleep be damned. He parked Millicent and her traveling gear, reclaimed from her room at the cost of twelve dollars in back rent, and his own bag and saddle at a restaurant near the railroad station and walked the short distance to the town marshal's office.

"Kyle," he said with relief as he entered the office he remembered all too well. "I'm glad to see you in this time. And I'm damn sure sorry about what happened to your young deputy here."

"Hello, Longarm." Lewis stood to greet him. The Cheyenne marshal was a tall man with a close-cropped beard and pale, searching eyes. They shook hands across Lewis's desk, and the local lawman motioned for Longarm to take a seat. "Thanks for your help that time."

"Look, I know excuses are feeble, and if I'd been paying more attention to what was going on that day—"

"I heard all about it from the witnesses," Lewis interrupted. "There wasn't anything more you could have done." He sighed heavily. "Sure shook up a lot of folks in this town, though. Perk was a good boy. If it's anybody's fault it's mine for letting him in here with a job he couldn't handle. But frankly, Longarm, I'd like to drop that subject. It doesn't set too easy and I'd as soon forget it."

"All right."

"I expect I can guess what you came to see me about."

Longarm nodded. "T. Anthony Scott, an informer named Mel or Mal, and a train robbery that's supposed to take place."

"What is it you want to know?" Lewis asked.

"Every damn thing, Kyle. Right from the beginning. There is something—I don't know what, but there has to be something—that I've missed in this business, because I've just come from Virginia City, and there isn't a damn thing stirring there."

Lewis leaned back in his chair and pursed his lips. "I'll tell you the truth, Longarm. I'd damn near—mind that I said *near*—stake my reputation on the idea that this Mal fellow was telling what he believed to be the truth. Can you think of any reason for anybody to lay a false trail about it?"

Longarm shook his head. "I've wondered about that myself. More than a little. Spent a lot of time on the train back here thinking about it, and I can't come up with anything. If somebody had it in for the Professor and wanted to get the law on him, they'd tell a straight story to make sure he was picked up and sent back to trial for murder. No point in lying about that since the man already had a stack of wants and warrants out on him thick enough to choke a buzzard.

"About the only person I can think of who might want

to lay a false trail for his own benefit would have to be the Professor himself. And I can't see that that would do him any good, either. No matter how big an opinion the son of a bitch has of himself, he isn't going to think he can draw off all the law officers in the territory and send them running to another part of the country. Posses don't come that big for William Bonney, much less a small-time crumb like T. Anthony Scott.

"I even wondered if he could have figured that I might get assigned to the case and want me sent on it so he could lay for me and get some revenge for me putting him in Leavenworth. But damn it, Kyle, if that was so he'd've had to have been there to do something about it when I arrived. And the man just hasn't been seen anywhere near Virginia City that I can learn about." Longarm shook his head again. "What it comes down to is, I just don't understand it. Now I want to start all over and take a fresh stab at it, right from the beginning."

Lewis took a rank-looking twist of near-black tobacco from his top desk drawer and neatly trimmed off a chew with his mouth and sat back, chewing reflectively for a moment. Longarm knew the man well and did not hurry him while he got his thoughts in order.

"From the beginning, then," Lewis said slowly. "It was on a Tuesday morning this fella came in here. Never saw him before. He was kind of mush-mouthed and I never did get clear on what his first name was, either Mal or Mel. Dressed like a hard-rock man. Lots of dust on his clothes. Brogans instead of boots. Cap instead of a hat. You know the type."

Longarm nodded.

"Named this Professor of yours. Powder man called Duck. Al Higgins. Leroy Tyler. Perk and me found the flyers afterward giving more information on Duck Bragg and Al Higgins. I expect Perk showed those to you."

"He did."

Lewis grunted and nodded. "Right, then. Let's see." He held a topless tin can to his chin and spat into it, then set it aside. "He said, and I think I can remember this pretty close to his own wording now, he said, 'They wanted me to go in with 'em on a train shipment heist. They said it'd be the biggest thing I'll ever get into. The train's goin' out the end of the month an' the Professor figures to take it as she runs down through the woods.' That's as accurate as I can remember that part of it, Longarm. I also got the impression—and here I cannot recall if he said it or implied it—but I got the idea that the timing had to do with the phase of the moon as well as the shipping date. Apparently the shipments are frequent enough that they could pick one dependent on the conditions of moonlight needed for whatever Scott had in mind. Although what that could have to do with anything, I do not know."

"Me neither," Longarm said glumly.

He sat back with his eyes closed and ran through his mind what Lewis had just said that Mal had said that his contact had said that...Shit, Longarm thought, pass the directions from Denver to the mountains through that many hands and even *they* could get fucked up, and the damn mountains right there in plain sight.

"He said the end of the month?" he asked Lewis.

"Uh-huh."

"And he said 'down through the woods'?"

"Uh-huh."

"You're sure."

"Pretty sure. I didn't have anybody copying it down or anything, but I'm pretty sure that's what the man said."

"Damn it, Kyle, that don't make the least bit of sense. 'Down,' for instance. That could mean south, or it could really mean *down*. The rails run north out of Virginia City, not south. And the whole country is up and down out there, but mostly you got to go either up or across to get anywhere by rail from Virginia City once you go north to Reno and

131

hit the main-line tracks. Either up into the Sierras or across into Utah. I can't see either way being called 'down.'"

Lewis shrugged.

"And 'through the woods,' Kyle. Hell, man, there isn't a patch of decent timber anywhere closer than the slopes of the Sierras. Everything's cut so short for shoring timbers and firewood that the jackrabbits have a hell of a time finding a place to hide. There's no woods within *miles* of Virginia City."

He got another shrug from Lewis and another stream of spit into the nearly full tin can. "I can't argue with you. I'm just telling you what the man told me."

"Another thing," Longarm complained. "You're sure he said it was *gold* they were after?"

"That part I'm sure about."

"Damn it, there isn't hardly any gold shipped out of Virginia City. It's all silver now. They told me the gold was mined off years ago and they don't take hardly any of it out any more."

"Don't snap at me about it, Longarm. I'm not the one that said any of this. I'm just the messenger boy."

"Sorry, Kyle." He smiled. "I guess I get a case of the red-ass when I'm this confused and frustrated." He pulled a cheroot out and nipped the end off with his teeth, then struck a match and lighted it. The rich smoke did not make him think any better, but it did make him feel somewhat better. He sighed.

"Kind of like I felt when I got to Torrington and learned the Calder gang was off in a completely different direction," Lewis said sympathetically.

"Yeah. Damn it." Longarm took the cigar out of his teeth and burped into a closed fist. "I . . . *oh, Jesus!*" He straightened in his chair and groaned.

"What?"

"Fools, Kyle. I've been one and so have you."

"What do you mean?"

132

"You said it yourself. A completely different direction. *We've been looking in the wrong damned direction.*"

"I don't understand you," Kyle Lewis said.

"Damn it, Kyle, this is exactly what happens when we get so damn smart we think we know what we're doing. This is exactly what happens when we go to making assumptions. Tell me, Kyle, where is Virginia City?"

Lewis looked puzzled and slightly annoyed. "That's a fool question, Longarm."

"Sure it is. But answer it anyway."

"Nevada, of course. Not far from Carson City."

"Of course it is, Kyle. Of *course*. That's my point exactly. Every damn body knows where Virginia City is. Virginia City, Nevada, and the Comstock Lode. Hell, everybody knows that."

"So?"

Longarm tipped his head back and laughed. "Don't you see, Kyle? *There is more than one Virginia City.*"

"Huh? I . . . wait a minute." Lewis sat up straight. He got an odd expression on his face for a moment, and Longarm wondered if he had come close to swallowing his chew. "Hell, yes. Montana. There's a Virginia City, Montana, too."

"Right. And *that* one fits. The rails run *south* out of Virginia City, Montana. Through timbered country. Right down to Denver.

"This Mal fellow didn't travel any thousand miles before he stopped to tell the law. He stopped at the first damn town he came to where he thought he could find a federal officer, or an honest one. But this right here is the first city of any size at all between here and Virginia City, Montana. And if I'm remembering right, it's gold they mine up there mostly, not silver like in Nevada."

"I will be damned," Kyle Lewis said softly.

"I will be, too, more'n likely. But in the meantime I've got to catch the first coach out to Virginia City, Montana."

133

Longarm stood and barely took time to shake hands goodbye before he was out of Lewis's office door and heading back for the restaurant where he had left Millicent Cater and their baggage.

For the first time since Billy Vail had given this assignment, Longarm felt some small degree of encouragement.

Chapter 17

Longarm fretted and fumed, but the powers of a deputy United States marshal were definitely limited. There was, for instance, nothing he could do to make the railroad lay on a special coach just to get him to Virginia City—the Montana one—any quicker. And there was no regularly scheduled traffic moving north until morning.

"It's all right, Custis—my goodness," Millicent tried to reassure him.

"It *isn't* all right," he insisted.

She took his arm and tucked in close beside him. She had to tip her head far back to look up at him. When she did so she gave him a wink. "Bet I can think of a way to pass the time, since we have to wait anyway."

He laughed. "All right." There seemed no point in pretending reluctance since Millicent was, after all, correct. They couldn't go anywhere until the trains moved.

Since they were already at the depot he took a few minutes to send Billy Vail the briefest of brief reports and to request that more expense money be wired to him at Virginia City, Montana. Then they went in search of a suitable hotel.

Longarm barely had time to deposit their bags in the room and lock the door behind them before Millicent was insinuating herself into his arms.

"Shy little wench, aren't you?"

"Um-hmmm." She stretched up to reach him and began nibbling on his lower lip.

"Tasty too," he observed.

"Um-hmmm."

"And talkative."

"Um-hmmm." She released her hold on him and dropped back onto her heels to turn and offer her back so he could help unhook the countless small buttons on her dress. It was a chore Longarm did not mind performing.

"Satisfied?" he asked when he was done.

She grinned. "Um-hmmm."

Longarm stripped while Millicent finished undressing. He lay on the bed and watched. She was down to her chemise and stockings and seemed to be enjoying the idea of putting on a show for his pleasure.

Millicent gave him another wink. She propped her foot on the edge of the bed beside him and took her time about unsnapping the stockings from her garter belt. She smelled of powder and perfume, and Longarm was standing at attention—selected portions of him, anyway—ready for her.

"Want some help with that, too?"

Millicent shook her head and grinned. She rolled the sheer material of her stockings slowly and provocatively down a well-turned leg, then did the same with the other leg.

"Tease," Longarm accused.

"Um-hmmm."

She pulled the chemise off over her head and tossed it aside. Wearing nothing but the garter belt now, she began slowly to unpin her hair, releasing it into a gleaming cascade that flooded down over her back and shoulders.

Longarm licked his lips.

She was a pretty morsel, he thought. Her breasts were

136

large, her nipples small and delicately pink. Beneath that impassive swell of firm bosom, her waist was narrow above a swell of rounded hip, and her belly had the velvet texture of flat planes that only youth can give.

Millicent turned away from him and began to brush her hair with tantalizing slowness.

"Aren't you ready yet?"

She turned and smiled. "Um-hmmm."

Longarm groaned. "Damn, but you learn fast," he told Millicent.

She gave him a cat-like grin. "Um-hmmm."

For perhaps five minutes—it seemed much longer—she had been happily kneeling between his knees. He had been hard to begin with. Now things were getting almost painful. If he didn't like it so damn much he would make her quit. But he had been correct. She *had* learned fast.

She bent over him again, and he could feel the softly curling ends of her long hair trailing lightly across him.

Her tongue laved his cock, and he groaned out loud again. Millicent chuckled.

She pulled his foreskin up to cover the head of his cock and slid her tongue inside the sheath to circle the head and excite him all the more.

Without warning she pulled away from him and, with a laugh of sheer delight, flopped onto her back at his side with her legs spread wantonly wide.

"Fuck me," Millicent whispered.

The words sounded odd, and oddly exciting, coming from her, in spite of what she had just been doing, and Longarm rolled on top of her eagerly.

Her small hands found him and guided him inside her. She was already wet and fully ready to receive him, and she raised her hips to meet his plunge.

"Hard," she whispered. "Take me hard and fast this first time."

He would have been more than willing to wait for her,

to delay his own release so she could reach hers, but her whisper was as much a permission as it was a request, and he obliged her.

He drew back and spread his knees slightly to steady himself, then grasped her roughly by the shoulders and lunged forward, driving deep into her with the full, hard length of his massive tool.

Millicent moaned, and her lips drew back from her teeth in a rictus of sensation as Longarm began to buck on top of her body.

She wrapped her legs around him and rode with him while he plunged again and again, slamming over and over into her belly and driving himself deeper and yet deeper into her moistly willing flesh.

She had built him so high already that much, much too soon he stiffened and groaned and clutched at her fiercely as the super-heated fluid spewed out into her receiving body.

He shuddered and collapsed onto her, and Millicent wrapped her arms around him and cradled his head to her.

"Um-*hmmm*," she said softly.

After a time Longarm rolled off her, and Millicent left the bed to go fetch him a cheroot and a match he could enjoy in the aftermath of their exercise. She snuggled close against him and cupped his balls in one small hand while he smoked.

"Nice," she whispered when he was done with the smoke.

"What?" he asked with a facetious grin.

Millicent took her hand away from his scrotum and poked him hard in the ribs.

"Oh. That."

"My turn now," she said.

"Sorry. You done wore the poor thing out."

"Hah! I know better than that, good sir. Don't forget, I've been to this well before."

"Have you? I disremember."

She poked him again, harder.

"Ouch, woman."

"Now do you remember?"

"Well, maybe I do at that."

She grinned and kissed him. She stroked him with lightly insistent fingertips, and almost immediately he began to rise to the renewed occasion.

He tried to press her over onto her back, but she resisted.

"Could you do something for me, Custis? If you wouldn't mind, that is."

"Maybe."

"I've . . . well, I've seen dogs do it, and horses and such. Would you mind . . ." Millicent blushed and got a shy expression on her pretty face. ". . . Well, mounting me?"

His answer was a grin.

Millicent got onto her hands and knees and turned her round, pretty rump to him. He knelt behind her and slid his glistening, still damp length into her. Millicent winced and pulled forward a little.

"Did I hurt you?"

"No, it's just . . . different. Wait. Let me. Ahhh-h-h-h." She backed up against him, this time accepting all of him into herself. "Yes." She wriggled her rump against him and sighed. "That's better."

Slowly, very slowly and gently this time, Longarm began to rock back and forth.

He reached around under her to find and to fondle the tiny, hard button at the edge of her vaginal lips, and Millicent began to groan. She pressed herself back against him.

With his other hand he found a breast and rolled its hard nipple between his fingers while he stroked slowly and insistently into her.

The gyrations of Millicent's ass became quicker, and he could hear her ragged breathing as she neared a climax.

Her flesh enfolded him and tightened in a convulsive reflex to grip him, and he could feel her shuddering and quivering beneath his hands.

She let out a short, yipping shriek and fell forward onto the bed, releasing him with a loud, wet plop as she collapsed limply onto the mattress.

Longarm grinned and lay down beside her.

He had not made it. Not this time, yet. But they were in no hurry. Their train would not leave for hours. And a man can get by on mighty little sleep when he has other things to distract him from it.

He waited, and soon Millicent rolled over with a smile of joyous satisfaction on her pretty face.

She reached for him.

Chapter 18

Kyle Lewis and Hank Bigelow were examples of what local law could and should be. County sheriff *and* Virginia City town marshal Reed York was an example of what local law too damned often was, Longarm decided within moments after meeting the man.

The fellow sat there, overweight, unshaved, and bleary-eyed, and scratched under his right arm while he yawned and coughed. Lice, Longarm thought unkindly.

The man wore a red wool union suit and bib overalls and had some kind of dinky little pistol shoved so deep into a cowhide pouch in his pocket that he would have to make an appointment to get the thing out if he ever needed it, which, Longarm also decided, he was unlikely to do. No wonder this was vigilance-committee country if York was the kind of law enforcement these poor bastards had to put up with. The man simply did not seem interested in what the federal deputy was trying to tell him.

"Wal, we shore 'preciate th' word, deppity," York said lazily, "an' we'll shore make certain nothin' comes of it.

141

You c'n count on that." He yawned and scratched his armpit again.

"Yeah. Thanks," Longarm said. He did not bother trying to hide his distaste for the lawman.

"You run on back t' Denver now an' tell your boss man it's all tooken care of."

"Yeah, well, I'd do just that, Sheriff, except I've been given an assignment here, so I'm kind of duty bound to see it out. I expect you can understand that." It was the most charitable way Longarm could think of to put it.

Unexpectedly, York showed a quick leer and a wink. "Reckon I can for a fact, deppity." He chuckled nastily. "I kinda heerd already 'bout the filly you checked into the Placer *Ho*-tel."

Longarm stiffened and his eyes went cold. York obviously saw the sudden change, because he cleared his throat and sat upright in his chair with a nervous, squirming motion. "I . . . uh . . ."

"Let me warn you about something, Sheriff. Miss Cater is indeed an acquaintance, but perhaps not the kind you assume. She is a newspaperwoman, Sheriff, and has been assigned to write an account of Virginia City and this attempted robbery." He leaned forward and said seriously, "I understand, Sheriff, that she has rather—shall we say *powerful* political and journalistic connections in the East. I am not at liberty to say more, you understand. But if I was you, Sheriff, I'd be real careful how I allow the little lady to be treated in my town."

York's fat face flushed, and he squirmed in his chair some more. "Do tell."

Longarm sat back in his chair and smiled. "Not me, Sheriff. I'm not supposed to tell a thing."

"Oh," the sheriff said weakly.

"Exactly." Longarm took out a cheroot and fired it up with a match from his coat pocket. "So what I'm going to have to do, Sheriff, to protect my own backside, is to make a show of being busy around here. Naturally, you can handle things just fine on your own, but U. S. Marshal Vail wants me to look busy here, so I'll have to nose around some too. You understand that, I expect."

"Oh, 'deed I do. Sure." Sheriff York looked unhappy.

No wonder, Longarm thought. If a true description of the man's competence ever got into the eastern papers, the whole damned mining camp would be a laughingstock. And while miners were normally men who could forgive a lot of human frailties, being laughed at was not one of the things they were fond of. A really good newspaper article on the law-enforcement situation in Virginia City would most likely lead to a sudden change of personnel, possibly by way of feathers and tar.

"Since you understand the situation," Longarm said, "I'll go on about my business here."

"Absolutely," York said.

"Good."

Longarm stood. The sheriff levered himself out of his chair, too, but Longarm managed to turn and head out of the office before the silly son of a bitch could get his hand out for a shake. There were some things, Longarm knew, that went beyond the call of duty. Having to be civil to Reed York must surely fall into that category.

He stepped outside the small, log-walled jail-and-office combination and stood in front of it to survey the town.

Compared with the other Virginia City, this one was something of a letdown.

Much smaller and infinitely cruder, Virginia City, Montana was a typical boom camp waiting to die as soon as the gold veins played out.

There were no sidewalks here, no elegant opera houses or fancy saloons. There were saloons aplenty, but like the other buildings on the streets they were false-fronted affairs thrown together out of tenting or native logs. As far as Longarm had yet seen, there was not a single stone or brick

143

structure in the entire community, and the streets were no more than meandering ruts, carved by use rather than design.

In spite of that, though, the camp had an air of busy, vibrant activity about it, and the streets and stores were full of life.

Pedestrians hurried back and forth through the streets, sidestepping rumbling wagons and no small number of pack animals. Obviously, Longarm thought, Virginia City served not only the adjacent hard-rock mines but far-flung placer diggings and prospectors as well.

That much activity certainly meant a corresponding wealth being drawn from the earth, he knew, and Virginia City would probably be ideal for the Professor's purposes. There was plenty of gold available for an intelligent thief to appropriate. Plenty of newcomers arriving and departing without notice to hide an influx of robbers. And it was plenty close enough to the Canadian border for Scott to slip away as soon as he had his hands on the loot.

It was, Longarm thought, too damned perfect.

The question now was how to stop the man.

The best way, Longarm realized, would be for him to locate the Professor and put him back behind bars before the robbery could be pulled off.

Behind bars or under the sod.

Longarm had no fondness for killing, but a man of Professor Scott's temperament would not be easily taken. With a murder conviction waiting for him back in Kansas and a noose quickly to follow, Scott was not likely to surrender himself. He would fight like a cornered badger, and Longarm was not looking forward to it.

Still, there was no point in putting things off. Longarm's experience had been that procrastination seldom made a bad situation get better.

Millicent had said something about seeking a story about a wild boom camp. She had already written an account of the affray back in the other Virginia City, which Longarm

144

had refused to read on the grounds he did not want to have to start disliking the girl, and had mailed copies to several large newspapers in the East. So she was out of his hair for the rest of the day.

He dropped the stub of his cheroot into the dirt and ground it out with the heel of his boot. Nope, he thought; there was no point in putting anything off. He felt to make sure his Colt was riding securely in its proper place and walked toward the biggest and fanciest saloon he could see on the busy street.

The bartender's reaction was pretty much typical of what Longarm was coming to expect here. When Longarm posed his questions, the barman delivered only a scowl and a sour beer. When Longarm produced his badge and made the question official, the bartender turned and deliberately spat a stream of brown juice into a handy cuspidor.

"You haven't seen anything, then?" Longarm asked.

"I ain't paid to see," the bartender said with a sneer.

"There's a reward involved."

"I've heard that before, so fuck off." The man turned and walked off behind his bar.

Damn, Longarm thought. Big help, these bastards. They all seemed to feel they were so far removed from civilization here that they were immune from any considerations of right or wrong, and any man could be as straight or as lawless as he wished.

Still, short of taking to beating every bartender in town in the hope of getting information that they might not even possess, Longarm could not think of an alternate solution.

Feeling grumpy, his belly churning from the ingestion of too many green-tasting beers drawn from too many suspect kegs, he headed back for the Placer Hotel, where by now Millicent should be waiting for him. He was feeling so gloomy that he was not even looking forward to her company, particularly since the walls of the rooms in the

Placer were nothing but canvas tarps suspended from a framework ceiling. Any activities more vigorous than a kiss and a wiggle would be overheard by half the men staying in the place.

Millicent was not in her room or in his, so he went next door to the café that was more or less attached to the Placer. The place was crowded and noisy, and it smelled of grease that had been used too hot and too often and of men who had bathed too seldom.

Millicent was there, seated at the end of one of the long, communal dining tables. She was surrounded by miners who kept giving her sidelong glances while they pretended to concentrate on their suppers. That was no wonder, Longarm thought, after the kind of women they would be used to seeing here. Millicent stood out among the rough-dressed men like a peacock in a cote of guineas.

There were no other women in the restaurant, and the only decently dressed man in the place was a slender, handsome young man who was sitting beside Millicent. Longarm was not sure whether he approved of the fellow being there to insulate her from the miners or if he was beginning to feel a pang of jealousy. While he watched, Millicent leaned toward the gent and said something, listened for a moment, and then laughed. Longarm frowned.

Millicent looked up and saw him in the doorway. She smiled and waved, motioning for him to join her—or them. Longarm forced the frown off his face and crossed the earth-floored room.

He would have jammed his way to a seat on the bench between her and the gent, but she scooted over toward the young man and made room for Longarm on the end of the bench.

"Custis, how fortunate you found us. I was just telling Barry about you."

"Really?" He wondered sourly just what she could have been telling him. Not everything, he was sure of that.

"Yes. Custis, this is Barry Field. Barry, this is Marshal

146

Long. Most people call him Longarm."

"My friends call me that," Longarm corrected.

"A pleasure," Field said. He half stood with his knees hooked behind the long bench that was serving that entire side of the table and reached behind Millicent to offer his hand. Longarm shook it with no particular pleasure.

"Custis, Barry is...what is it exactly now, Barry?"

"Special Investigator for the Mine Operators' Association," Field reminded her.

"Oh?" Any budding jealousy was forgotten now, and Longarm leaned forward to get a better look at Field. He did not mind, though, that Millicent's small hand slipped into his beneath the table and gave him a squeeze.

Field was slightly built and dressed like a dandy. He was clean-shaven and looked no older than Millicent. But there was the bulge of a shoulder holster under his suit coat and a predatory look of self-confidence in the pale, smoky gray of his eyes.

Maybe this association of his knew what they were doing when they hired him, Longarm judged.

"I didn't know you had a Mine Operators' Association," Longarm said.

Field smiled. "They aren't a noisy bunch like the cowmen seem to get," he said, obviously referring to the bold-as-brass Stockmen's Association down in Wyoming, where "range detective" was just another name for assassin. "But they know what they're doing," he continued.

"Maybe they're the people I need to talk to, then," Longarm said.

"Miss Cater was just telling me something about that."

"Oh?" He was going to have to have a word with Millicent later, in private. For some reason he kept forgetting that one of the principal attributes of a journalist, even a would-be journalist like Millicent, was that they tended to have loose tongues. It probably was all right that she had brought his assignment up in conversation with Barry Field, assuming young Mr. Field really was what he represented

147

himself to be, but a word in the wrong ear could be deadly to Longarm or, worse, to Millicent herself, if the Professor got his hands on her and decided she knew more than she really did. That thought was a worrisome one.

"I'd like you to tell me more about what you've heard, Marshal," Field went on, "but I don't think this is the appropriate place for such a discussion. Nor," he added, "the appropriate company."

Field made it a point to look around at the miners who were still stealing frequent glances toward Millicent. Certainly the threesome was the center of attention in the place.

Longarm got the impression, though, that Field, wisely enough, may have included Millicent in that reference. Longarm hoped that he did. If so, it could mean there would be some competent help available from the association, even if there never could be from the local law here.

"You're right, of course, Barry."

"May I suggest, then, that we adjourn to the association's headquarters? I think it will be more to your liking, Marshal."

"Of course."

"You haven't eaten yet?"

"No."

"Good. Miss Cater and I were just having coffee. And I think we can find something interesting for our dinner, perhaps a cut above the meals they offer here."

Damn near anything would accomplish that, Longarm thought, judging by what he could see on the tin plates along the table.

When they reached the association's building, though, it turned out they would have had to travel a long way to equal, much less exceed, the fare that was offered.

The headquarters was more a private club than the offices Longarm had more or less expected. It was a huge, three-story structure on the edge of town. Although it was built of logs, like nearly everything else in Virginia City, it was furnished with taste and with money.

148

They dined in a large room with polished floors and a bandstand on one side. Field explained that the dining room was also used as a ballroom at times.

The meal was excellent, oysters and pâté as well as perfectly cooked steaks and a selection of pies and pastries for dessert. Longarm stuffed himself, and Millicent seemed to thoroughly enjoy the dinner, too, although she ate with ladylike reserve. When Longarm asked for their bill, Field informed him that only members and association officers had use of the facilities and that no charge was made.

Afterward Field introduced Millicent to several of the mine owners' wives, who were playing cards in another room. Before she could object, he left her there with a brief explanation that he and Longarm would retire to the smoking room.

"Very neat," Longarm said as Field guided him to a small sitting room and closed the doors behind him.

"Thanks." Field motioned the federal deputy to a deep, leather-upholstered armchair next to a now cold fireplace and turned toward a sideboard where decanters and stemmed glasses were waiting. "Brandy?"

"Rye is more to my taste."

Field examined the brass plates held by thin chains around the necks of the decanters. "Bourbon is as close as I can come."

"That'll do, then."

Field poured a bourbon for Longarm and something else for himself, then settled into a matching chair nearby. He toasted Longarm with a raised glass. "To a successful conclusion, Marshal."

"I can drink to that." The bourbon wasn't Maryland rye, but it wasn't entirely rotten either. It sure beat the swill the local saloons served in the guise of beer. Longarm rolled the smooth, obviously very old liquor on his tongue before he swallowed it. "You lead a rough life around here, Barry."

"As a matter of fact, Marshal, sometimes we do. As I suspect you already know, any time one man has something

149

there is going to be some son of a bitch hanging around who wants to take it from him. So I would really like to hear more about this tip your people got."

"All right, I'll make a deal with you. I'll tell you about it if you call me Longarm instead of by a title."

Field smiled. "Deal."

Longarm sketched in the facts as he had heard them from Kyle Lewis.

When he got to the Professor, though, Field's face went pale, and the young man leaned forward in his chair. "This man's name, Longarm. What was that again?"

"Scott. Professor T. Anthony Scott. He's wanted under federal warrants for mur— Say, what's wrong, Barry? Do you *know* the Professor?"

Field groaned. He drained off the rest of his brandy at a gulp and went to the sideboard for a refill for himself and one for Longarm, apparently forgetting that he and Longarm had not been drinking the same thing.

"You do know something about him, don't you?" Longarm asked again.

"Son of a *bitch*," Field answered.

"That bad, is it?"

"Worse than bad." Field shook his head and took another jolt of the brandy. "A week and a half or two weeks ago we were approached by a Professor Scott Anthony."

"That do sound familiar," Longarm said. "Gives him an out, too, if somebody calls his name by mistake, damn it. I told you the man wasn't stupid."

Field nodded unhappily. "Like I mentioned before, Longarm, ours is a quiet organization. We don't like for even our own miners to know everything we do, which probably explains why this informant of yours didn't say anything to me about the plan. Naturally he couldn't go to our sheriff, but if . . . well, never mind that. It's too late to be concerned about things that are too late to change."

Longarm nodded.

"Anyway, Professor Anthony—Professor Scott, more

than likely—had certainly heard of us. Oh, Jesus, I hate to admit this part of it . . ."

"Too late to change that too, I'd guess."

Field nodded. "What happened was that this Professor came to us representing himself as a principal in the Chicago Vault and Security Company, Incorporated."

"Uh-oh."

"It gets worse. I hadn't ever heard of the company, but that was hardly surprising, and he had a bag full of printed materials and letters of recommendation and, oh, I don't know what all else. It all *looked* legitimate, Longarm."

"I told you the bastard was smart."

"You better believe it. Anyway, what he wanted to do was to sell us a security consulting service and all the hardware needed to meet his recommendations."

"You mean he wanted to get you to pay him for his time while he cased you for a robbery?"

Barry Field looked utterly miserable. He nodded.

"Did you?"

Field sighed. "Guilty." He took another hefty swallow of the brandy. "I told him I didn't think we could use any vaults or tricky locks, considering the amount of bulk involved when we ship concentrate, but I'd be interested in his recommendations. Besides, I said, it probably wouldn't be ethical, or anyway wise, to buy hardware from a consultant. But I did want his recommendations. Oh, *damn* it, Longarm." Field put his snifter down and buried his face in his hands. "I showed him *everything* and paid him a hundred dollars' retainer against a five-hundred-dollar consulting fee when his report is delivered."

"What I think we'd best do," Longarm said gently, "is have a little discussion with your Professor Anthony before my Professor Scott pulls off his robbery."

Chapter 19

The Professor had rented a small house on the outskirts of Virginia City. It was shared, Field had heard, by several associates, although the association investigator had never met any of them. It was easy enough for both men to conclude that the silent "associates" also living in the house would be the other members of the Professor's gang.

"Bunch of bastards," Field complained.

"It's going to be all right, Barry. At least we know where to find them. We can wait until late, time enough for them to get drunk or whatever they like to do in the evening. Then we can pop in and round them up."

"Damn right we will," Field said with determination.

Longarm did not blame the man if he wanted to take this personally now. After all, he had been hoodwinked rather well by the crafty Scott. Field should be eager to get Scott into custody before the man could make use of his association-supplied knowledge.

"We need more men than just the two of us," Longarm said. "If possible, I want to take these birds alive. And, alive or dead, I damn sure don't want the Professor getting past us."

"I'm the only investigator the association employs," Field told him, "but I can call on the security men from any of the member mines. If you think we'll need them I can have fifty men here within an hour, and all of them as tough as they need to be."

"A dozen should do it, I think. Too many and we risk creating a mob. I won't have that, Barry. I want you to know that. We take them alive if possible. So bring in men with something better than mutton between their ears."

Field nodded. He looked grim. "You can wait here for me if you like. I'll be back in an hour with your posse."

"It might be better if I see Miss Cater back to the hotel," Longarm suggested. "I assume she'll be safe there."

"There wouldn't be any problem with that. There's a lot of good men among the miners. No one could bother a respectable lady without getting his arms ripped out . . . among other things."

"All right. I'll see you back here in an hour."

The men Field had gathered were a rough-looking crew. Rough enough that Longarm would not willingly face them down himself if he had any say in the matter.

He just hoped they were as controllable as Field promised. This was, after all, vigilante territory, and Longarm did not want to have to report back to Billy Vail that he had created a bigger problem than he had been sent here to solve.

"What we want to do," Longarm told the group before they left the association building, "is to surround the house before we tip the gang that anything is up. That is important, boys. We have to be quiet until everybody is in position. Mr. Field will assign you to your places when we get there. Remember, quiet is the word.

"When you are all in position, Field will report back to me, and I'll start the ball rolling. I have a warrant here for the arrest of the Professor, and I intend to serve it. There are warrants outstanding on some of the other men as well, but we'll have to sort that out after we get them all. In the meantime, I want each of you to remember this: no shooting—*none*—unless they try to break past you or if they shoot first. Otherwise—well, we're going to try to do this quietly all the way through. If they know they are surrounded there's at least a chance they will give themselves up. Far as I know, the Professor is the only one of them facing a hanging, so there is a good chance they'll surrender. If they are willing to give up, let them. You all have handcuffs?" He waited and got a round of nods from the hard-looking men who were gathered in the small room with revolvers at their belts, and most of them with shotguns in their hands as well.

"All right," Longarm said. "Mr. Field will lead the way and put each of you into position. Stay sharp. And good luck to you."

The men filed out of the room without comment or commotion. That was a good sign, Longarm thought. They seemed like a seasoned crew and not afraid of a scrap if and when it came to one.

Field led the group and Longarm trailed along behind. He was satisfied with the way things were going. It all seemed easier, in fact, than he had any right to hope for. After his own display of stupidity, as he preferred to view it, going to Nevada when the problem was in Montana and the delays that had caused, it looked like for a change he was going to be able to nip a robbery in the planning stages instead of having to chase a criminal down after the fact.

Just how a judge might view a preemptive attack was still in doubt as far as the planned robbery and the other gang members might be concerned, but with that warrant in his pocket charging Scott with the murder of a Leavenworth guard there was no question that a federal deputy had jurisdiction here. Whatever else did or did not happen tonight, Scott was not going to walk away from an arrest on

154

the basis of a legal technicality. Something like that bothered Longarm more than just about anything else could, and he was glad to know that he had that covered. And once they had the Professor, he really did not much care what happened to the rest of them.

It was satisfactorily late by the time they made their start from the association headquarters. It had taken Field more time than he had expected to gather his posse and still more time to arm them all and find handcuffs for them to carry. Longarm was not all that sure the group could properly be called a posse, actually, but he was not going to quibble about petty details.

The men had seemed amused by the idea of carrying cuffs. Longarm got the impression their accustomed style would have been to beat a man senseless if they wanted him to hold still. But the deputy had insisted on that. If he had anything to say about it, this roundup would be conducted with all due respect for law and propriety.

Field led them through the night for more than a mile. Some of the men had grumbled about having to walk the distance, but Longarm had been worried that horses or wagons would cause too much noise and he had insisted on them all going afoot.

It was sometime past two o'clock in the morning when they finally reached the vicinity of the Professor's rented house, and Longarm was relieved to see that the house was in darkness, with no lamps showing light through the windows. A sleeping man was much easier to surround and take, and Longarm still had fond hopes, if few expectations, that he could accomplish the arrests without any bloodshed.

The windows were open, he saw, so he moved up to Field's side and whispered, "Make sure you have all the windows spotted and covered as well as the doors, and have at least two of the men lay back and keep a watch on the roof. There could be some way out, or they could force one quick enough, and I wouldn't want any of them to get away from us."

Field nodded and led his men off into the night. The men were security guards, not woodsmen or sneak thieves, and they made more noise walking than Longarm would have liked, but he knew, too, that his own keenly attuned ears and worried anticipation made him much more sensitive to sound at the moment than a sleeping gang member could possibly be.

Longarm pulled his Colt from the holster and by habit checked the cylinder to make sure it was loaded and ready. As the arresting officer, it was up to him to approach the silent house and inform its occupants that they were being taken. At such close quarters, his rifle would have been useless, so he had left it back in the hotel room with Millicent, who had argued to no avail that both she and the rifle should accompany Longarm for this conclusion to her story.

Field returned, alone now, and let out a low half-whistle under his breath to warn Longarm of his approach. "The boys are in position, Longarm," he whispered.

"All right. You slip around to the back door then, Barry, and I'll beard the lion at the front. Go ahead. I'll give you a minute's head start."

"Right." Field disappeared into the darkness. Although, Longarm noticed, the darkness was not all that complete. It was not yet a full moon, but there was plenty of light in the cloudless sky from what moon there was. Field, he saw, was good at moving silently and with stealth through the darkness. Even knowing where he was and where he was going, Longarm had difficulty keeping the young investigator in sight.

Longarm waited the minute he had promised, and then another, just to make sure Field would be ready. Then he slipped forward toward the dark house looming in front of him.

He felt a flutter of nervousness as he reached the door, and his juices began to flow. Long experience, though, told him not to worry about it. Whatever came, he would be able to handle it. And if the day ever came when he did not believe that, that would be the day he would have to look for another line of work.

Longarm stood in front of the closed door. He adjusted the set of his Stetson and wished fleetingly for a cheroot. He took a fresh grip on the familiar butt of his Colt and pounded as hard as he could on the door with his left fist.

"Officers of the law," he said loudly. "Open up and surrender yourselves."

For a moment there was no sound at all. Then, from somewhere on the far side of the house, a rifle fired.

That one shot was all that was necessary to set off a regular battle.

Rifles and shotguns ringing the house began to explode, and chunks of lead were lashing at the log walls all around Longarm. Bits of flying bark and splattered lead nipped at his clothing, and he threw himself down and backward.

"Damn it!" he yelled. "Damn it!"

All the firing he could see or hear was coming from *outside* the house, and he was fairly sure that that first shot had come from his own posse, too.

He did not believe there had yet been any return fire from the Professor or his men.

"Cease fire. *Cease fire!*" Buckshot tickled the sleeve of his coat, and he quit yelling and began to scuttle the hell out of the way.

All around the house Barry Field's posse of security guards was pouring lead into the still dark and silent place.

"Damn it, I said to *cease fire.*"

Longarm began to stalk from man to man, slapping their gun muzzles down and hollering at them over the thunder created by the others. With two of the men he had to snatch their rifles from them before he could get them to stop shooting.

"Cease *fire*, damn you!"

157

Eventually they were all quiet, and Longarm stood among them, glaring from one man to another. "Didn't I tell you all . . . ah, forget it."

Disgusted with the lot of them, he turned and stomped back to the door he had had to vacate in the face of his own men's fire.

"I told you boys you're under arrest," he yelled. "Do you believe me now, or do you want another demonstration?"

There was no answer.

"Barry?" he called.

"Yeah?"

"Do you hear anything inside?"

"No."

The suspicions Longarm already held had grown to a near certainty now, but it never paid to be foolish about an unproven belief. He thought about breaking the door in, then had another thought and tried the latch before he went to the bother.

The house was not locked. The door swung open at his touch.

Uh-oh, he thought.

He stepped inside and flattened himself against the front wall, listening intently for any hint of movement or breathing.

"Shit," Longarm mumbled.

Emboldened by anger now, Longarm stomped his way forward through the strange room until his boot toe connected with a piece of furniture. It was a chair. He felt beside it and found a table. On the table he felt a lamp.

"Son of a bitch!" he muttered. He reached into his pocket for a match, lighted first the lamp and then that cheroot he had been wanting.

Colt in one hand—he was positive the place was empty, but not *that* positive—and lamp in the other, the cigar clenched between his teeth, he investigated each room in the place.

The lamp would have been visible from the outside, and after a moment he heard Barry Field's call.

"It's all right. No, damn it, it *isn't* all right, but you can come on in anyhow. The bastards've flown."

He heard Field dismiss the posse. A moment later Field joined him inside the house.

With the lamps lighted, the effects of the unnecessary gunfire were evident.

Windows were shattered and draperies torn. Mirrors were broken into glittering shards, and the furniture upholstery was torn and gauged. The wallpaper had been pocked with numerous holes where lead was embedded into the walls.

"Kind of a mess, huh?" Field asked.

"Yeah."

"The owner won't be happy with this."

"You know him?" Longarm asked.

"Yeah."

"You aren't going to like this, but..."

"I know. I know. The association ought to pay for the repairs." Field sighed. "I wouldn't mind that, you know, if we'd just gotten the damned Professor. But..." He sighed again. Longarm wanted to do the same.

"It woulda been real nice if it had worked," Longarm observed.

"Real nice," Field agreed.

The two wandered through the house, checking the drawers and wardrobes, but apparently the Professor and his men had left nothing behind.

"I'd have to say," Longarm said, "that it looks like they've cleared out for good. But why now?"

"They must be close to pulling their job," Field said.

"That would have to be my guess, too. A few last-minute preparations, maybe, and then bam, they've got you."

Longarm went over to the fireplace and stood with his elbow propped against the mantle. The globe of a lamp had been shattered there but by some miracle of happenstance the oil reservoir was unharmed. Idly Longarm began to tidy the broken glass into a pile with his free hand.

"Barry."

"Um?"

"I found a note under this glass here. The envelope has your name on it."

"You're kidding."

"No, it was right here on the mantle. Must have been propped up against this lamp that got busted."

Field tore it open, read it, and then, with an expression of disgust, handed it to Longarm.

"Mr. Field: Your assistance and personal kindnesses have been deeply appreciated. By the time you read this you shall be aware of my expertise on the subject of our mutual interest: *i.e.,* gold shipment security for the M.O.A., which you so ably represent. I shall forward to you at the earliest opportunity my final report and recommendations. You may, however, consider my fees already paid in full. Thanking you for your cooperation, I am, respectfully yr's, T. Anthony Scott, Prof."

"That son of a *bitch*," Field groaned.

"Maybe not," Longarm said. The federal deputy was grinning. "By the way, Barry. What were those 'personal kindnesses' the Professor thanked you for?"

Field gave him an anguished look. "I'm the silly bastard who found him this house to rent."

Chapter 20

It was three o'clock by then, but Longarm was wound too tight to think about sleep and he suspected that Field was feeling the same way. By unspoken consent they walked back to the Mine Operators' Association building. The place was closed and locked—the gentry here did not keep the same hours their workers did—but Field let them in with a key and took Longarm upstairs to the executive offices.

"Have a seat," Field told Longarm. He poured brandy for both of them, which Longarm accepted without complaint. There were more important things than a choice of liquor to think about at the moment.

Field produced a copy of the association's shipment schedule from a locked safe and handed it to Longarm. "I guess it won't hurt for you to see this," he said. "Hell, the Professor has, so why not you, too." He sounded bitter. "I suppose," he added, "what we'll have to do is call a session of the association board tomorrow and make sure this schedule is changed. I expect they will want my resignation, too. It was a good job while it lasted."

"Maybe you ought to keep it then, Barry," Longarm said mildly.

Field gave him a dirty look.

"And I don't think you ought to change anything about the shipping schedules, either."

"What is this—your turn to help the Professor?"

Longarm smiled at him. "What we have here," he said, "is more than the association's schedule. It's the Professor's schedule, too. And, personally, I'd like to take that bastard in."

"But . . ."

"Think about it, Barry. Whatever the Professor has in mind, whatever he had to go off early to arrange, he wouldn't have risked leaving that note for you unless he expected to take the very next gold shipment you have on this schedule. The man has already demonstrated pretty well that he's no fool. He isn't going to leave something like that lying around where it could be found in time to tip you. And that has to mean he's ready to move right now."

Longarm looked first at the calendar hanging on the office wall, then down at the list in his hand.

"Tomorrow night, Barry. That one has to be it. The train pulls out at dusk, and if I remember correctly the moon won't rise for a couple hours after that. The informant told Kyle Lewis that moonlight was one of the requirements, for some reason, so that means the robbery won't take place for some distance down the track. I'd say we have to be getting close to pinpointing the time and place even if not the method yet. What do you think?"

Field shrugged.

"One thing, though," Longarm went on. "I don't understand the figures you have on your list here so I can't judge if the dollar amounts are enough to justify the Professor's planning."

"The figures are in numbers of boxes," Field explained. "Each member mine operator lists the number of boxes he expects to ship on a given date. You'll notice that not all

162

mines send concentrate in a given shipment, though. This one..." he referred to the list Longarm was holding "...this one has five mines shipping on that train. One, four—" He added the figures swiftly. "A total of eighteen crates are scheduled to go out tomorrow night."

"What would that be in dollars?"

Field shrugged. "We aren't talking about placer dust here, which is nearly pure, but an ore concentrate made from a mercury evaporation amalgam process. It has to go to a mint or a licensed refinery before it's made into pure bullion or a less pure jewelry-grade metal. Your average concentrate is worth roughly twenty dollars an ounce. Troy ounces, that is; a dozen to the pound. And there's fifty pounds of concentrate to the shipping crate."

Longarm pursed his lips and let out a low whistle of astonishment. "Nine hundred pounds of the stuff. That'd be... what?" It was simply too mind-boggling for him to be able to figure it quickly.

Field shrugged. "I couldn't tell you exactly without seeing specific assays from each batch of concentrate, but you can call it two hundred thousand, or a bit more if the productions are average."

"Damn," Longarm breathed softly. "Half the owl-hoots this side of the Mississippi would kill a man for fifty dollars. What would they do for a piece of that kind of money?"

"Anything the Professor told them to," Field said. "Absolutely anything."

Longarm took a swallow of the brandy, so preoccupied that he did not even mind the taste of it, and at least the stuff did warm his belly. "We have to remember," he said, "that the Professor is planning to take all this concentrate somewhere. That means he has to move nine hundred pounds of dead weight somehow. Tell me about the crates."

"Wood. Two-inch stock. Bolted together, not nailed or screwed. Strapped with bar iron that is welded shut. There are also eyes welded onto the straps so the individual crates can be chained and locked to the floor of the rail car. We

163

don't want pilfering en route by anyone, including our own guards."

"That means it can't be any hit-and-run operation. They would need time to cut or break the boxes free after they stop the train, and that would add to the weight of the crates, too. Since they would have to plan on speed from their pack animals, I'd guess they'll use mules. Probably no more than one crate to the side of a pack frame. That means nine mules. Good ones. Then haul ass—no pun intended—for the Canadian border. Take them—what, four days? Possibly more, depending on their route."

Longarm shook his head and drained his glass. "I don't know that I like that, Barry," he went on. "They can count on a number of hours to make the transfer from car to mules if they can stop the train and kill everyone aboard, sure, but in a hell of a lot less than four days they'd have a posse hot after them. So they'd have to pick an evasive route, which would take more time to reach safety and increase their risk by that amount. I just don't know that I like the way it shapes out. For sure, though, the Professor has come up with something sneaky and totally unexpected. That right there is what worries me the most."

"Stopping the train . . . well, anybody with a prybar can do that," Barry replied. "Tear up the track and that train is going to stop, regardless of our intentions. But killing everybody aboard would take some doing, Longarm. The Professor knows about the guards we carry. Four men locked inside the car with the crates of concentrate, each of them armed with sawed-off shotguns. A sandbagged gun perch on top of the car with those short-barreled field artillery model Gatling guns mounted to cover either side of the railroad right of way and additional mounting posts front and rear in case anybody tries to come over the top of the cars to reach them. Gun nests on the tops of the cars in front of and behind the gold car, in case somebody thinks he can blow the gold car and kill everyone in it that way.

164

I just don't see how they could do it, Longarm. I really don't."

"The Professor does."

"I know."

"That's another thing," Longarm said. "This Duck Bragg is known to be a powder man. So whatever Scott has in mind, it involves explosives."

"Dynamite?" Field asked.

"I don't know. I know Bragg is expert with giant powder, but I don't know about the more modern stuff. Higgins is a muscle man, in charge of moving the crates once they're available, I'd guess. The others I don't really know about. They'd need a lot of firepower to face the kind of security you've described, that's for sure. But according to the information this Mal fellow gave Kyle Lewis, they aren't putting together an army. Just a robbery gang. *Damn*, I wish I knew what Scott has in mind."

"We'll find out tomorrow, Longarm."

He nodded. "Look, Barry, it's up to you, of course, but I worry about a thief as smart as the damned Professor. If I were you, I think I'd lay on the full complement of guards, but no more than that. And just to play it safe, I'd ship lead in those strapped and welded crates. Don't tell anybody that you don't absolutely have to, and ship it like it was the real thing."

"I agree. And I intend to be on that train, Longarm."

"So do I, Barry. So do I."

The short freight pulled out on schedule, just as the sun was sinking out of sight to the west. The association guards were in their normal places, with shotguns loaded and Gatlings fitted with racks of gleaming .45-70 cartridges.

Armed as they were, Longarm knew that the guards were capable of withstanding an assault by anything short of a regiment of regular troops . . . and even they would probably need artillery support to overcome the amount of resistance

165

those Gatlings could pose.

Yet Scott *knew* about the Gatlings and quite obviously he was not concerned about them.

Damn the man, Longarm thought for perhaps the thousandth time in the past few hours.

Neither he nor Field had had much opportunity to sleep during the past day, and Longarm knew that fatigue had taken the edge off his abilities. And he would need to be at his best during the coming night.

Millicent, meanwhile, was grumbling and complaining about being left back in Virginia City, when to get the real flavor she needed for her article she wanted to be on the train.

It was a good thing the fool woman didn't have any money, Longarm thought, or she would probably buy a ticket on the single passenger coach the train was hauling.

He and Field were riding in the caboose, the car immediately behind the gold car with its bait of lead-filled crates. Field had wanted to ride inside with the crates, but the car doors were bolted and locked from the outside as soon as the crates and the guards were securely loaded, and Field could not afford to be trapped inside the car when the Professor made his move.

At least, Longarm thought, the brakeman in the caboose was keeping the stove fired and a pot of coffee readily available.

The slat-sided little car was comfortable enough, too. The benches were padded, and there were cooking facilities and bunks on board in the tight-cramped space. Overhead was the glassed-in observation chair where either Longarm or Field would be riding at all times.

Since the brakeman would not be able to keep his usual station there to watch for lantern signals from the engine, Longarm had rigged his portable telegraph key to a sending set and operator in the engine. The man and key had been provided at the association's expense.

There were no high passes to be negotiated, so the train

166

was pulled by a single engine. The trip up from Cheyenne had shown that there were many medium grades to be climbed, though, as the train made its way south through hilly, wooded country toward the grass flats of Wyoming and the arid desert of that territory's midsection.

The train rocked rhythmically south and east once they reached speed, clicking swiftly over the joints in the rails. Longarm was seated in the observation tower with his rifle and a borrowed shotgun on a shelf close to hand.

"Coffee?" Field asked, stepping up into the open perch beside Longarm's left leg.

"Sure."

Field brought it and said, "While there's still a little daylight I'm going to go forward and check on the men."

"All right."

Field let himself out onto the platform at the front of the caboose and climbed the ladder to the top of the gold car, where the primary gun nest was situated. There was a backup nest to Longarm's rear, blocking much of his vision in that direction, although that seemed unlikely to be important. The other backup nest of sandbags was on top of the passenger coach. Beyond that there were only the wood tender and the engine. Longarm had been too busy to watch the passengers board the coach, but he hoped there were not many of them. He did not like to see civilians exposed to danger, but he had not had the authority to order the coach left vacant. Besides, he realized, that could tip the Professor that they were aware of his scheme—some of it—if he was bright enough to have a man watching the departure for him. And telegraph wires, as Longarm well knew, can be tapped by anyone with a key and a little knowledge.

He decided he would be damned glad to see dawn come around again.

Field walked forward on the roof of the gold car to talk with his gunners there, then hopped to the roof of the passenger coach and spoke with the men in that nest. Instead of returning immediately, though, he climbed down the ladder on the back of the coach and presumably went inside it. He looked unhappy when he returned.

"What's up?" Longarm asked.

"While I was up there I happened to think I'd better take a look at the passengers. See if I recognized anybody as a possible ringer, in case they want to have somebody on board to help their plan."

"And?"

"Three drummers, a miner's wife and kid, two men that I recognized and figure should be all right... and Miss Cater."

"How...?"

Field looked sheepish. "This afternoon she asked me if she could get a rail pass from the association so she could go down to Yellowstone and do a story on the national park there. The association has pass privileges because of the amount of traffic we generate. And, well, I guess I let her have one."

Longarm's jaw worked and he wanted to tell the young man that this was one mistake too damned many. But it was too late for that. Millicent was already on board the train, riding happily into the teeth of a potential disaster.

Damn Field, Longarm thought. It was part of the job to put oneself in danger. But to be so stupid as to allow a girl to be endangered too... *Why* hadn't he cleared it with Longarm, damn him?"

Longarm clenched his teeth and kept his mouth shut, but his expression probably made clear what his feelings were.

As a matter of fact, at this point, after having been so helpful to the Professor and so stupid about Millicent, Barry Field's judgement was in doubt. The man might or might not have the makings, but he damn sure did not have the seasoning his job needed at a time like this.

All of which, Longarm quickly realized, was just a way of avoiding the truth, which was that he was a hell of a lot more responsible for Millicent Cater than Barry Field was.

168

He should have checked on her but he had not. If anything happened to the girl now it would be his responsibility at least as much as Field's. That thought did not make him any happier.

"Take over up here, Field," he said curtly.

"Yes, sir." The response popped out automatically, even though the federal deputy had no real authority over either Field or this operation.

Longarm dropped down out of the observation tower, and the association investigator climbed up into it.

"Keep an eye out for downgrades," Longarm warned him.

"Down? It's easier to stop a train on an upgrade."

"I know, but I've been thinking about that. If they only wanted to stop it, sure. But the Professor is also going to have to kill everybody on board or at least injure them bad. He could get a worse wreck on a downgrade where you can't brake worth a damn even if the engineer spotted something in time."

"All right, then."

Longarm's first inclination had been to go forward and raise hell with Millicent for her stubborn stupidity in coming along. But it was too late for that now, so he quickly calmed himself.

Instead, while he thought about it, he sat at the tiny table whose surface folded down from the car wall and tapped out a message on his key to the operator in the engine, warning the engineer to disregard his schedule time and proceed with extreme caution on all downgrades. The operator receipted the message, but Longarm had no way of knowing if the engineer in charge of the freight would comply with his request or not.

With that out of the way, Longarm contented himself with another cup of coffee from the pot on the stove and poked around in the caboose for something to read.

He would have been happier, really, if the lamps in the

169

car had all been extinguished so his night vision would be better, but he did not want to do anything that would depart from the normal operation and appearance of the train.

Regardless of what else happened, he did not want to spook the Professor. He wanted that man. He wanted him tonight.

Chapter 21

Longarm was bored. The brakeman was a silent, brooding fellow who seemed to resent the intrusion of his betters into his domain, and he seemed too dull-witted as well to have any interest in reading. Longarm would have welcomed a *Police Gazette* or a *Harper's* to pass the time with, but he had made the mistake of assuming there would be reading matter in the caboose.

The only things written on paper he could find, in fact, were a pile of train orders and a map. He idly unfolded the map and began looking at it, trying to decipher just where they might be from the infrequent mileposts and running signals they passed. The railroad's version of a map first baffled, then intrigued him, and for the time being his boredom was forgotten.

After a while Barry Field came down from the observation tower and helped himself to coffee. Longarm, already annoyed with the man because of the rail pass he had given Millicent, gave him a cold glance.

"It should be all right for a while now," Field explained. "We've hit level ground until we cross the river."

Longarm looked down at the map he had been studying. "What river is that?"

"The Yellowstone. We're right about...here." Field pointed to the spot.

"Really? Hell, I was twenty miles off. Are you sure?"

"Positive. I've made this trip a lot of times, Marshal."

Obviously, Longarm realized, the engineer was making better time than Longarm had thought. The man must not have been heeding that advice about the downgrades, or they could not possibly be approaching the Yellowstone already.

"I think...Oh, Jesus!" Longarm leaped up from the bench and knocked Field aside on his leap toward the table holding his telegraph key. "How close are we to the river?" he hollered.

"I don't know." Field looked puzzled. "A couple miles, maybe."

Longarm was no longer listening. He was frantically tapping on the telegraph key.

It took the operator in the engine an agonizing amount of time to response to the call.

HALT, Longarm signaled. IMMEDIATE HALT EMERGENCY.

He turned to the brakeman and yelled, "Set your brakes, man. Now!"

The brakeman gave him a bored look. "I don't take my orders from you."

"You do tonight, damn it." Longarm grabbed him by the shoulder and yanked him off his seat by main force, propelling him toward the platform and the screw-wheel that would set the mechanical brakes on the car.

"All right, all right," the brakeman said grudgingly, but he went.

The tempo of the clickety-clatter over the rail joints changed, began to slow.

"What the hell is going on here?" Field demanded.

"The Yellowstone, Barry. Look at it on the map here.

Remember any geography of this country? The map doesn't show it all, the scale's too fine, but the Yellowstone flows *north* from here to the Missouri, damn near all the way to Canada. It's navigable, too, more or less. And what's an even easier way to haul heavy loads than pack mules? Water, man. *Float* the stuff. Nine hundred pounds of gold, man.

"Think about it. Unless I'm wrong, the Professor will be waiting up at that bridge span with his men and a boat or a raft. Maybe even some mules to lay false trail with. That's the way I'd plan it. Lay a false trail for your posse to follow and take the gold north on the river.

"Hell, an ambush there is about the last thing a man could expect, too. If I remember right, that span has a long approach on this side before it crosses the water, right?"

Field nodded.

"So they wait until the train is just about to the span, maybe even out onto it a ways, and they blow the bridge. That would be Bragg's part.

"The train drops onto the ground below. Nobody would live through that, either. Right there, man, all these guards and security precautions are nullified. Everybody dead or hurt so bad they couldn't raise a hand to defend themselves. A couple of the Professor's boys take care of the survivors with shots in the back of their heads. The rest take their time about cutting the crates out of the busted freight car. They load the crates onto their boat and drift off while somebody else leads a bunch of mules away to lay the false trail—straight north toward the border, say, or if he's really feeling devious, back toward Idaho first and then north. Meantime, the Professor is floating away, clean and clear. Hit the Missouri and offload onto some more mules, and go to Canada. He could do it. The son of a bitch could actually get away with it."

Field looked skeptical, but by then the train had slowed. Brakes squealed as they were screwed down tighter to apply more drag against the massive inertial weight of the rolling train.

173

It took, Longarm knew, half a mile or more to stop a train, much more if the speed or the load were great.

The question was not so much whether they could stop in time, though, as whether they could stop far enough away from the bridge for the Professor not to realize his plan had been discovered. That was what Longarm wanted.

The train came to a shuddering halt finally, and Longarm leaped out to run forward toward the engine.

The engineer was on the ground and coming back toward the caboose already. He looked angry.

"Why the hell did you stop me, Marshal? You better have a good reason or the road will have your badge for this."

"Is avoiding a wreck a good enough reason?" Longarm asked.

"It would be, if you was right. How do you know?"

"I know. Just take my word for it or we'll spend half the night arguing." Longarm did not *know*, of course, but this hardly seemed the time to admit that to the engineer. Better if the man accepted Longarm's guess as gospel.

"Now what?" the engineer asked grumpily.

"Wait here. I'll get to you in a minute."

Members of the train crew were beginning to gather around, and so were some of the men from Field's security force. Longarm called the men down from the Gatling nest, too.

"All of you security men," he said, "get your small arms and come with me. Leave the Gatlings in their mounts. They're too bulky to carry."

"We can't just leave the gold like that," one of the men protested.

"You can if Special Investigator Field tells you to," Longarm said. "Besides which, there's no gold in that car. It's a decoy."

The men looked as much angry at the deception as they did curious about the stop. Longarm knew he needed to keep talking so they would not begin to act on their anger.

174

"We'll leave four men here in case the train has been seen to stop and they send someone overland to raid it. The four men inside the gold car can do that. You, unlock the door and let them out. They're probably worrying about the unscheduled stop. You, go up and tell that telegraph operator that I want to see him."

Millicent and most of the passengers had joined the confused group now. Longarm took one of the guards by the arm and pulled him aside from the others. "You, you see that lady there?"

"Yes, sir."

"She's your responsibility for tonight. Keep her inside that passenger coach even if you have to handcuff her to a seat. Do you have cuffs?"

"No, sir."

"Here." Longarm handed the man a set of steel cuffs and gave Millicent a warning glance. From her expression he knew she believed that he meant it, and she resented that belief.

But if it was a question of keeping her safe or letting her continue to care for him—well, he could get along without her good will easier than he could get along with the knowledge that he had let her come to harm.

"You," he said to another guard. "This train doesn't move until I say it does. If the crew doesn't like that, too bad. Tell them to take it up with the federal government. Understood?"

The man looked to Barry Field, who was standing quietly in the background, for confirmation of the orders.

"Do what the marshal says," Field told them. "All of you."

"Good. The rest of you gather up your rifles and shotguns. We have a hike to take."

One of the men groaned. Longarm remembered him from the surround of the empty house the previous night.

"That's right, I like to walk a lot. It's good for you. Get some of that gut worn off. And this time I don't want any of you men to turn trigger-happy like you did last night. You in particular, mister." He pointed to the man who had been doing the complaining.

"Get your guns now, and let's take us a bunch of train robbers." Longarm ran back to the caboose to get his Winchester.

The men were assembled and ready within minutes.

"We'll have to hurry," Longarm said. "We don't want them to think we can't keep a schedule." He led them down the tracks toward the trestle span over the Yellowstone.

The Professor had planned well, he thought. There was plenty of moonlight to light their way. Perfect for finding scattered crates of gold and navigating a rocky river. Perfect as well for leading an ambush party against the ambushers.

"Spread out now. Both sides of the track. And injun forward slow and quiet. They'll be on this side of the span, likely down below that rim above the river. They won't be expecting us, and I don't want you to let them know we're onto them until it's too late. Understood?" He was speaking in a whisper and could only hope that all of the men could hear him.

They were halted at the end of the timber that flanked the tracks here. Beyond lay a hundred yards or more of open ground, then an abrupt slope down toward the river level. It was somewhere on that slope that Longarm expected to find the Professor and his men.

With any luck, that is. He still had seen nothing that would prove his theory about the Professor's robbery scheme. It was all hunch and guesswork at this point, but he had to act on it. Being wrong here could lead to some embarrassment and a waste of time. It could even lead to the loss of his badge, if the railroad really got mad about it.

But being wrong in the other direction, taking the train across the bridge without investigating it first, could lead to the deaths of several dozen men and women. Longarm would not risk that.

"Spread out now and move forward in a skirmish line."

The association men did as they were told, and within minutes they were moving carefully forward.

At least, Longarm thought, the Professor would not be expecting anyone to approach on foot. He was waiting for the sounds of a steam engine to alert his men.

If he was there.

Longarm slipped forward silently, wishing the other men had learned to be as quiet. They were out of the timber, but many of them were still managing to find sticks and twigs to stomp on. Longarm wondered if the damn fools had brought some along with them for just that purpose.

They reached the beginning of the slope and started down.

Longarm knew that was the most critical time, when the association men would be silhouetted against the sky while the Professor's gang waited below.

Without warning, Longarm's hunch was proven correct.

"Hey!" someone shouted. "Up there!"

Bright lances of gunfire erupted in the night from a point halfway down the slope. From the top the dark mass of shadow there had looked like a small thicket. Instead it turned out to be a group of men. The moonlight was enough to show them scatter as they shot.

The association men dropped to the ground and began to return the fire with vicious volleys of rifle and shotgun fire.

Directly below him, not more than fifty yards away, Longarm could see another, smaller cluster of men. He ran toward them. Barry Field was running beside him.

Someone in the second group fired at them, and Field grunted and fell.

Longarm whipped the Winchester to his shoulder and sent a low, searching pattern of shots into the group. They spread out, but one of the men fell. Another bellied down behind a magneto-powered battery box of the kind used to set off explosive caps.

Longarm was close enough to see both the man and the

battery box clearly now. It was more than enough to confirm his suspicions. The charges would already be in place on the bridge span, and all it would take to destroy the bridge would be a single thrust of that plunger. It had to be Bragg, because Longarm could see now that the man had a peg leg and could not have fled on foot. Bragg reached up for the plunger handle.

Longarm stopped and took a moment to aim the Winchester. He touched off the trigger, and Duck Bragg flopped back away from the battery box.

There, Longarm thought. That ought to make the railroad happier. Replacing bridges was likely not something they wanted to do.

He ran forward and stopped long enough to make sure that Bragg was dead and to take a quick look at the other man who was on the ground. Whoever the man was, Longarm had never seen him before. He was not the Professor.

Off to the side, beyond the trestle structure, the association men were waging a furious battle with the Professor's gang, but Longarm thought there was less shooting coming up the slope than there had been.

Where the hell was the Professor, though?

Two men had fled from beside the battery box. One of them must be the Professor. But where were they now?

They would not have run toward the gunfire to the left, and Longarm thought they had darted in that direction. So where . . . ?

Of course, he thought. The shadows under the bridge. But which direction would they have taken then? Up, to flee on foot? Or down?

He smiled. He had been right so far. It followed, then, that there should be a boat down on the riverbank. That was where the Professor would be heading. Longarm plunged down the slope at a breakneck pace, barely able to keep himself from overbalancing and falling forward onto his face from the impetus of his own hard run.

He felt his feet start to get away from him as he broke

out of a thin screen of brush onto the riverbank, and to avoid a headlong tumble he deliberately slid down onto his hip with the Winchester held protectively high.

Someone shot at him from the edge of the water as he went down, but the bullet whistled harmlessly overhead.

Won't give 'em but so many chances, old son, Longarm thought.

He brought the Winchester down level and, one-handed, snapped a shot off at the dark figure beside the river.

The bullet connected, by luck as much as by design, and the men fell into the swirling flow of the fast-running Yellowstone.

The second man was already in the boat and was trying frantically to get the craft cast off away from the shore.

He stopped what he was doing long enough to take a shot at Longarm. He missed.

Longarm came to his feet. He could see the man fairly clearly. He was wearing a swallow-tailed coat and opera hat; he almost *had* to be the Professor.

Longarm's Winchester swept upward toward his shoulder just as the Professor shot again.

The Winchester saved Longarm's life.

Coming up across his chest toward his shoulder, it took the Professor's bullet just in front of the machined steel action. The lead slug smashed into the rifle and whined viciously off into the night.

The impact sent the rifle crashing back against Longarm's chest, driving the breath from his lungs and numbing his hands with its force. He stumbled and barely caught himself from falling.

The ruined and useless Winchester fell from his numbed grasp, and he reached for his Colt, only to find that his hand did not have the strength to grip the revolver.

He had to stand in idle frustration as the Professor threw back his head and laughed.

"Is that you, Long?" he called.

"It's me, Scott. You're under arrest for murder."

179

The man laughed again and raised his rifle for another shot. There was nowhere on the rocky riverbank for Longarm to hide.

The current grabbed at the floating boat and turned it, throwing Scott's aim off. His bullet went wide.

Roiled and eddied by underwater rocks, the current tossed the boat violently, and the Professor had to sit down abruptly to keep from being thrown overboard. He clung to the sides of the boat. He looked at Longarm across the gap that was quickly widening between them and laughed again.

"Goodbye, Long."

Longarm tried again to palm his Colt, but there was still no feeling in his bruised hand. He had to watch impotently while Professor T. Anthony Scott picked up an oar and fitted it into a lock to act as a sweep so he could guide his boat through the turbulent water.

"Look me up in Canada, Long," Scott called.

Which meant, Longarm decided, that Scott was *not* heading for Canada. Damn him. Or maybe he was, confusing the trail by deliberately telling Longarm exactly where he was going so Longarm would not think to look in that direction. Or maybe... Longarm shook his head. With the Professor, it could be any damn thing. Anything at all.

The gunfire beyond the trestle had nearly died now. The association men seemed to have everything under control there.

But meanwhile the Professor was floating happily away.

Longarm heard a shot uphill from where he stood and turned. The second man by the battery box, the one Longarm had thought was dead as well as Bragg, was on his feet. He was shooting uphill toward where Barry Field had fallen.

The light was good, considering, and Longarm could see clearly from the riverbank.

Field rose to his knees and aimed a revolver toward the gang member who had shot at him. Field's gun spat a gout of yellow flame, and the man stumbled. He turned and tumbled forward.

Onto the upright plunger of the battery box.

His weight drove the plunger down, past the line of magnetos inside the bulky, misnamed battery box.

An electrical charge sped along the wire that had been laid, and a hundred yards away there was a sheet of flame and an oddly low, hollow rumble of sound.

Two spans of the trestle collapsed and sagged to the earth.

Slowly, its support removed, the rest of the long bridge began to collapse as well.

Longarm turned to watch it fall.

He heard a scream, a totally unexpected sound, and looked in time to see that the Professor's boat was not yet clear of the bridge.

The Professor, screaming, was flailing the already boiling surface of the fast river with his sweep, but the power of the current was infinitely greater than any feeble efforts he could make with a single oar.

The boat sped inexorably downstream as the bridge crumbled above it. The Professor lashed the water with his oar, but all he succeeded in doing was to turn the boat sideways to the current as the immense weight of the railroad trestle collapsed on top of his frail craft.

The last Longarm saw of him was the Professor standing in the stern of his boat, fist raised and curses streaming from his lips, as massive timbers and iron rails rained down over his head.

The bridge spans hit the river surface with a hissing roar, and the Professor was lost under a gigantic splash that glistened silver in the moonlight.

Longarm stood for a moment, kneading his right hand with his left, trying to get some feeling back. Then he turned and began walking up the slope toward the wounded Barry Field.

There was still a lot of work to be done this night, and it would take some time for the engine to back all the way up the line to Virginia City.

Longarm felt damned tired as he climbed up the bank.

Chapter 22

Longarm propped his boots onto the front edge of Billy Vail's desk and lighted a cheroot. "Pissed, aren't they?" he asked.

"The railroad? Yes, I think you could reasonably say that they are pissed. Something about people not disconnecting battery boxes when they have the chance."

"At the time it seemed like there were more important things that needed doing," Longarm said evenly.

Vail cleared his throat and frowned. "Field judgement is not always that accurate, Deputy."

Longarm shrugged. "I reckon you're right, of course." He grinned. "Is it easier to be right, Billy, when you make your decisions after the fact, from the point of view of a desk?"

Vail coughed and looked away. Longarm decided he had made that point. It would be better not to push it any further. By way of explanation he added, "I tought Bragg and Higgins were both dead, Billy, and I thought it was important to try and take the Professor. If I screwed up . . . well, I'm sorry. I did what I thought best at the time. Now I can see that I was wrong. If you want my badge—"

"I don't want your badge, Longarm." Vail grinned. "The railroad does, I will admit that, but they can't have it."

"Thanks."

"I only keep you on, you know, because I'm afraid you might go bad if I cut you loose from the law. You have a devious mind, Longarm. You'd make a hell of a outlaw."

"Am I supposed to take that as a compliment?"

"If you like."

"I'm not sure, really. Let me think on it some. I don't suppose anything has been heard of the Professor."

"No. Not yet. The telegrapher did get your message through before the wires went down, of course, and all the agencies downstream were alerted to watch for a boat or a body. No one has found either. Are you *sure* the man is dead, Longarm?"

"I don't see how he could be anything but otherwise. On the other hand, I never saw his body either. Take it for what it's worth, Billy, whatever that might be."

Vail sighed. The United States marshal did not like loose ends any more than his best deputy did, but there seemed nothing either of them could do about this one until or unless Professor Scott's body washed up somewhere along the banks of the Yellowstone, or possibly even the Missouri.

"There is one other little matter, Longarm." Vail took a folded newspaper from his desk and flopped it open for Longarm to see.

"All the way from Boston, huh?"

"Uh-huh. All the way from Boston. There is another all the way from New York. And a third all the way from Philadelphia. And . . . do you want me to go on?"

"All that many, huh?"

"All that many," Vail agreed. "And all bearing the byline M. L. Cater. I take it you are acquainted with M. L. Cater, Longarm?"

"We've met."

"Is she pretty?"

Longarm grinned. "How'd you know?"

"How long have we worked together now?" Vail asked.

"I get your point."

"I do hope, Deputy, that collaboration with journalists is not something you intend to adopt as a habit. And you may take that as a warning."

Longarm took his boot heels down from the boss's desk and sat up straighter. "Yes, sir."

"Is M. L. Cater in Denver now, Longarm?"

"No, sir. She stayed in Virginia City to nurse a sick friend. I would say that she doesn't particularly like me any more, sir."

"I am glad to hear that, Deputy. I really am."

"Yes, sir."

"That will be all, Longarm. Report back in the morning. *On* time, if you please."

"Yes, sir." Longarm stood and turned to go.

"Oh, yes. I almost forgot. There is one other thing, Longarm," Vail said.

"Yes?"

"A Miss Savoit stopped in here looking for you. I promised to deliver a message. She said her troupe will be in the city through Monday next. She sent her regards and invited you to call if you returned before then."

Longarm grinned and tugged his Stetson down onto his head at a jaunty angle.

"Longarm."

"Yeah, Billy?" he asked.

"Be on time tomorrow morning. *Please.*"

Longarm was whistling a suddenly remembered tune as he left the office and walked lightly down the steps of the federal building to Colfax.

Here they are again!

LONGARM AND THE LONE STAR BOUNTY

Jessie, Ki and Longarm join forces for the third time!
Don't miss this action-packed novel featuring all three
of your favorite western heroes

coming in February!

Also, look for

LONGARM AND THE JAMES COUNTY WAR

sixty-third novel in the bold
LONGARM series from Jove

coming in March!

LONGARM

Explore the exciting Old West with one of the men who made it wild!